"There's a long way to go with this place, isn't there?" Jaclyn's voice was quiet, almost solemn. She stood, waiting for his answer as he locked the building.

"It'll be tough, but it can be done."

"You have enough on your plate. I don't want to add to your burdens, Kent."

"I want to make this clinic happen, Jaclyn. I see it as sort of a rallying point for the people of Hope."

"You do? How?"

"Your clinic isn't part of the old system. It's new, different. Maybe it can help undo past damage and end some of the bitterness. Maybe that's God's plan in all of this."

"Thank you for saying that, Kent. I admit I was a little discouraged when I came here tonight, but I feel reenergized now. You can't know how much that means to me." She stood on tiptoe and brushed her lips against his cheek. "You're a wonderful man, Kent."

If only Kent could have a chance to start fresh, like Jaclyn. He'd do so many things differently.

Maybe if he worked hard enough on her clinic, he could finally rise above his regrets.

Books by Lois Richer

Love Inspired

This Child of Mine
*Mother's Day Miracle
*His Answered Prayer
*Blessed Baby
†Blessings
†Heaven's Kiss
†A Time to Remember
Past Secrets, Present Love
††His Winter Rose
††Apple Blossom Bride
††Spring Flowers,
    Summer Love
§Healing Tides
§Heart's Haven
§A Cowboy's Honor
§§Rocky Mountain Legacy
§§Twice Upon a Time
§§A Ring and a Promise
Easter Promises
"Desert Rose"

‡The Holiday Nanny
‡A Baby by Easter
‡A Family for Summer
‡‡A Doctor's Vow

Love Inspired Suspense

A Time to Protect
**Secrets of the Rose
**Silent Enemy
**Identity: Undercover

*If Wishes Were Weddings
†Blessings in Disguise
**Finders Inc.
††Serenity Bay
§Pennies from Heaven
§§Weddings by Woodwards
‡Love for All Seasons
‡‡Healing Hearts

LOIS RICHER

began to travel the day she read her first book and realized that fiction could take her to places she'd only dreamed of going. Through reading, an ordinary day was transformed into an extraordinary adventure. Creating that adventure for others became Lois's obsession. Now, having written more than 40 books with three different publishers, Lois had been nominated three times for a prestigious Holt Medallion. With millions of books in print around the world, Lois continues to enjoy creating stories of joy and hope for Love Inspired Books. Married for almost thirty years, their two sons grown, Lois and her husband live in Canada but winter in Arizona. Their love of traveling makes it easy for Lois to find the perfect setting for her next story. Lois loves to hear from other readers. Contact her through www.loisricher.com or loisricher@yahoo.com or friend her on Facebook.

A Doctor's Vow

Lois Richer

Love Inspired

Recycling programs
for this product may
not exist in your area.

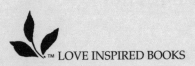 ™ LOVE INSPIRED BOOKS

ISBN-13: 978-0-373-87767-6

A DOCTOR'S VOW
Copyright © 2012 by Harlequin Books S.A.

The publisher acknowledges the copyright holders
of the individual works as follows:

A DOCTOR'S VOW
Copyright © 2012 by Lois M. Richer

A COWBOY'S PROMISE
Copyright © 2010 by Harlequin Books S.A.

www.LoveInspiredBooks.com

Printed in U.S.A.

Dear Reader,

Welcome to Love Inspired! We're celebrating our 15th anniversary this month, and you're invited to the party!

Love Inspired Books began in September 1997, offering readers inspirational contemporary romances. Fifteen years later, Love Inspired has never wavered from our promise to our readers; we are proud to publish short contemporary romances that feature Christian men and women facing the challenges of life and love in today's world.

In honor of our anniversary, we are showcasing some of our top authors in September. Irene Hannon, Arlene James and Lois Richer were part of the original lineup in 1997, and we're supremely blessed that they are still writing for us in 2012. Jillian Hart and Margaret Daley have been part of the Love Inspired family since the early 2000s. And newcomer Mia Ross rounds out the month. We hope you enjoy these sweet stories full of home, family and love.

As a special thank-you to our readers, each book this month contains a bonus story. Give them a try, and we know you'll find our authors the very best in Christian romance!

Thank you for reading Love Inspired.

Blessings,

Melissa Endlich

Senior Editor

This book is dedicated to the One who makes
dreams come true and does so far beyond
what we can ask or think. Thank you, Father.

* * *

Search me, O God, and know my heart;
test my thoughts. Point out anything you find in me
that makes you sad, and lead me along the path
of everlasting life.
—*Psalms* 139:23–24

Chapter One

Fire!

Pediatrician Jaclyn LaForge quickly ushered her patients out of her brand-new clinic to safety. Her relief was short-lived when the clinic's nurse grabbed her arm.

"Randy McNabb and his mom haven't come out," RaeAnn whispered. "I think they're still inside."

The volunteer fire department of Hope, New Mexico, wasn't here yet and Jaclyn wasn't going to wait for them. She kicked off her high heels.

"Wait," RaeAnn begged.

"No child left unattended, RaeAnn. That's our motto." Jaclyn raced inside the building, praying Randy and his mom were safe. Surely God would answer this prayer.

Inside the clinic, she moved from room to room. When choking black smoke enveloped her, she dropped to a crouch, calling Randy's name as she squeezed her burning eyes closed. Reopening them, she saw nothing. Her hand clutched air. Her lungs gagged on thick heavy smoke. She ripped off her jacket and held it over her face, trying to stem her terror.

Jaclyn reached for a shadow and knocked something over. She knew she couldn't stay in the clinic, but when she rose to move ahead, shards of broken glass pierced her foot. She collapsed in pain.

Don't let me die, God. Not before I've kept my promise to Jessica.

A gloved hand curled around her arm. Another nudged her jacket away from her mouth to plant a mask over her face.

She lifted it. "Randy—"

"Keep it there," a gruff voice ordered. "And hang on to me."

Jaclyn obediently inhaled the pure, clear air in gasps. Her rescuer heaved her over a very broad shoulder and carried her through the building. For the first time in years Jaclyn relinquished all control and allowed someone else to be in charge of her life.

As they emerged into the sunny spring warmth, Jaclyn pushed away the mask and inhaled, forcing her burning lungs to clear as she shot a prayer of thanks heavenward. Her rescuer gently set her on the ground. She lay still, overwhelmed by what had almost happened.

"Are you nuts? You don't go into a burning building. Not ever." The fireman in front of her ripped off his headgear and glared at her, his lips tight in an angry frown. But his fingers took her pulse with gentleness. He carefully eased her sooty jacket from her hands and tossed it away before checking her for burns. "Can you breathe okay? Do you need more oxygen?"

He tried to replace the mask but she pushed it away.

"I'm fine." Well, that would be true if her stomach hadn't just flipped in reaction to his touch. Jaclyn peered into cobalt-blue eyes and wondered who he was.

"Why would you go into a fire?" he demanded.

"A little boy—Randy—" She blinked at the familiar bellow that came from her left. "That's him. Where was he?"

"He and his mom used the old fire escape on the side of the building. They're fine."

"Good." She kept her gaze on the fireman, fighting not to look at her clinic. "I'm fine, too." She accepted his out-stretched hand to help her stand, winced and quickly sat down again. "Except for my foot. I stepped on some glass."

The fireman called for a first aid pack, shredded what was left of her stockings and examined the soles of her feet with a tender touch.

"I took off my shoes, you see," she said, as if that would explain everything.

"If those are your shoes, I'm not surprised you got rid of them." He shot a scathing glance at her spiked heels lying not ten feet away. "I don't know how you can even walk in those things." He glanced up, his blue eyes darkening to navy. "This is going to hurt."

"It already does. Go ahead." Jaclyn leaned back on her elbows and watched him delicately remove bits of glass from her foot. She tried to ignore her pulse-thudding reaction to him by trying to remember where she'd seen eyes so richly blue before.

Her rescuer's forehead pleated in deeply tanned furrows. So he was an outdoors guy, good-looking with the kind of massive shoulders that not even the bulk of a fireman's jacket disguised. He'd shed his headgear to reveal a face that appeared chiseled from stone.

His jaw clenched and unclenched as he worked, a tiny tic in his throat betraying his concentration. His hair—dark, almost black—lay in a ruffle of tight curls against his scalp—

"Kent?" Jaclyn whispered in disbelief. "Kent McCloy?"

"Yeah?" He lifted his head, blinked at her.

"I didn't recognize you. It's me. Jaclyn. Jaclyn LaForge." She waited. But Kent only nodded once and went back to work on her foot. "Thanks for getting me out of there."

"No problem. It's what firemen do." His drawl, like his face, gave nothing away.

Oh, no, her soul groaned. Kent was just like the rest of Hope's biased locals who couldn't believe the former bad girl of Hope could be a real doctor. Jaclyn was sick of that attitude. As if a mistake from her past made her completely unqualified to actually treat patients.

Kent squeezed the arch of her foot in preparation to draw out yet more shards. The last one was large enough to make her yelp in pain.

"Sorry." His fingers belied his gruff tone as he gently held her foot and poured antiseptic over the wounds. He began to wrap her foot in gauze—his bandaging skills were as good as or better than hers. "Okay?"

"It's fine." Actually his touch was more than fine, which was utterly confusing because Jaclyn had never reacted like this to anyone ever.

"I think I got it all but you should have somebody at the hospital check." He set her foot down and tied off the gauze. "No stitches needed, though I suspect it will be painful for a while. And wearing those shoes? No way."

Who cared about shoes? Jaclyn caught a glimpse of her dream—Jessica's Clinic—and groaned.

"It's ruined," she whispered, swallowing tears that would make her look weak. "It's totally ruined."

"Yeah, fires tend to do that." Kent offered a hand to help her rise. When she was upright, he slid his arm around her waist, as if he understood that only force of will and his help kept her standing. If he hadn't been there she'd have burst out bawling.

"But how could a fire start?" She looked from him back to the blackened, smoking building. "I had the place checked out. I had everything very carefully checked out."

"Then somebody missed something. Or it's an accident."

He shrugged. "Sorry, but the place is toast. In my opinion it isn't salvageable." Despite his harsh assessment, his blue eyes glowed with sympathy.

Jaclyn didn't want sympathy. Forget Kent McCloy with his midnight eyes, big broad shoulders and the gentlest touch she'd ever felt. Her dream was going up in smoke.

"I just opened." Despite her best efforts, a tear slipped out and trickled down her cheek. "I worked so hard to make this dream come true."

"Then you'll start over." Kent turned her to face him, his voice softer. "It's just a building. Compared to your life, losing a building doesn't matter. Besides—" he waved a hand "—Hope is full of empty buildings. I should know. I own that one over there."

She nodded, recognizing it. "Your dad's old law office."

"Uh-huh." He shook his head. A faint smile tugged at his mouth for a millisecond before it disappeared. "You can start over, Jaclyn. Take your choice of where." He waved a hand, as if it were simple to start again.

She blinked, surveyed the street then twisted to look at Kent again. If he wanted her to reopen he couldn't be holding her past against her. Maybe he'd even help her.

"Many of these places look worse than the one I was in."

"Probably are. Unoccupied buildings deteriorate fast." He turned away as one of the other firemen came over to speak to him. "She's okay. She should be checked out at the hospital for smoke inhalation. I removed the glass in her foot."

"Fire department volunteers aren't supposed to render that much first aid," the other fireman reminded, eyes dancing. "At least that's what you said at our last meeting, Chief. I can see why you did it, though." He gave Jaclyn a smile that should have made her heart throb.

Jaclyn wanted to tell him to save it for someone who would appreciate it, that she was devoted to her work—except for when Kent McCloy made her pulse race by taking glass out of her foot.

"Generally we don't. Do first aid, I mean." Kent's tanned face turned a shade of burgundy.

"Just couldn't help yourself this time, huh?" the fireman teased.

"The fire, Pete?" Kent reminded, dark brows lowered.

"Under control. But I'll take the hint and get back to work." The other man left smirking.

"What did he mean you couldn't help yourself? Are you a doctor, Kent?" Jaclyn frowned. "But I met the local doctors. At least, I thought I had."

"Vet," Kent corrected with a mocking smile. "I can't stand to see things hurting, though I usually treat a different species."

"Oh." She glanced at her foot. "Well, maybe you should broaden your practice. I'll be a reference if you like."

"You want me as competition in town?" His chuckle made her stomach quiver again.

"I'm not sure it would matter much," Jaclyn mumbled. "I could hardly have fewer patients." She gulped, regrouped. "It's good to see you again, Kent. It's been a long time since we were in high school together. We'll have to catch up sometime." She'd been so focused on the clinic she'd met hardly anyone—it would be nice to have a social life.

His beautiful smile disappeared, his face tightening into an unreadable mask.

"Sure." He looked around as if he wanted to avoid further conversation. "The ambulance is here. You'd better go with them, get your foot checked." His arm left her waist.

"I'm fine." Jaclyn studied him as she balanced on her uninjured foot, feeling suddenly bereft. "Have you lived in Hope since high school?"

"No." Kent's response didn't invite further questions. He

turned his head, nodding when one of the other firefighters motioned for him to join them. "I have to go."

"Well, thanks for saving my life." She waited until he'd taken a few steps away. "Kent?"

"Yes?" He turned back, his impatience to get back to work clearly visible.

"Was anyone else hurt?" She held her breath as she waited for his answer.

"Just you." He studied her for a moment longer, then grabbed the gear he'd thrown down and strode away looking larger than life.

Not that he needs any help there, she thought noting the badge at the top of his sleeve. "Fire Chief Kent McCloy is already the stuff of heroes. But that doesn't matter to me," she said aloud, as if convincing herself. "I have no time for relationships. I'm not back in Hope for a high school reunion."

So what was with her reaction to him?

"Jaclyn, you're talking to yourself." RaeAnn frowned. "How much smoke did you breathe in?"

"I'm fine."

"No, you aren't. Your foot is injured. For once, stop trying to be in control." RaeAnn slid an arm around her waist for support. "I'm taking you to the hospital."

Maybe they could get her head examined while she was there, Jaclyn mused. She checked over her shoulder one last time and saw Kent motion for another fireman to direct his hose on the back of the now-smoking building that had housed Jaclyn's clinic. That clinic had been the focus of her dreams for more than ten years. It was the place where she was finally going to earn the life she'd been given. The life Jessica had lost.

Why? That was the question that always haunted her. Why had her twin sister gotten leukemia and not her? In all the years since Jessica's death, she'd never figured that out.

"Ready?"

Jaclyn shook off her stupor and concentrated on getting into RaeAnn's car while her assistant retrieved her shoes. It must have been smoke addling her brain that made her notice Kent's broad shoulders again because Dr. Jaclyn LaForge was not interested in men—especially not Kent McCloy, no matter how good he looked in his gear.

Guys like Kent, even though they're gorgeous, have no effect on me, she thought as she sat alone in a treatment room, waiting to be examined by a colleague. But all the denials in the world couldn't disguise the way her heartbeat had raced when Kent had touched her.

How was it that the only guy she'd ever had a crush on in high school—the guy who'd stuck by her when everyone else had turned against her after Jessica's death—still had the power to make her shiver?

Didn't matter. Overpowering reactions notwithstanding, Jaclyn had no time for personal relationships. She had a duty to her twin sister to get the clinic up and running again. Despite losing the building, she would find a way to do it—no matter what.

Kent left the fire hall late in the afternoon after learning the fire was the result of an overtaxed electrical outlet. Thankfully no one had been seriously hurt. But the incident reinforced his long-held belief that it was time to get an emergency procedure plan in place in town.

He took his time driving home, surveying the land in its burgeoning spring glory. The last rays of sun sank below the craggy tips of New Mexico's mountains, bathing the world in a rosy glow as he drove into his driveway. It should have made him feel peaceful. But the usual post-fire adrenaline surge had left Kent antsy. He walked around the yard and thought about the town's new pediatrician.

Kent had forgotten a lot of things about Jaclyn LaForge since their days in high school—that silver blond hair of hers, for one thing. Then she'd worn it long; now her short, precise blunt-cut caressed a chin that said she was all business. The silky strands cupped her face, drawing attention to her delicate cheekbones and big brown eyes framed by long lush lashes. How could he have forgotten those lashes?

The pediatrician oozed class, from her red silk suit to her spicy perfume. Jaclyn, the rebel teen whom he'd known so well had been totally erased.

In an instant he time-traveled back five years.

"Kent, slow down. I can't keep up with you wearing these heels."

His wife would have envied Jaclyn her fancy shoes—they were the kind Lisa loved but said she could never wear in Hope.

"This is Hokey Ville, Kent." Three years later and Lisa's accusing voice would not be silenced. *"You said we wouldn't stay. You promised we'd go back to Dallas."*

A promise he'd made but never kept.

Uncomfortable with the memory of his betrayal, Kent clenched his jaw. Rescuing Jaclyn from that burning building had knocked his world off kilter. He doubted he'd ever forget seeing her through the smoke, but he needed to restore his carefully managed equilibrium because blocking out the past and focusing on the present was how he got through each day.

Oreo, his old Springer spaniel, strolled up to him and rubbed against his knee. Her white-and-gold patches gleamed from the brushing he'd given her this morning. As usual, the dog seemed to sense his mood. She nuzzled under his hand until it rested on her head, then laid her head on his knee.

"Did you get the pups straightened out, girl?" he asked. Oreo's daughter had given birth to ten pups the week before. Grandmother Oreo seemed to think it was her duty to ensure each one of the offspring received equal attention from their mother.

The dog's responsive yowl made Kent laugh. Her throated growls sounded as if she was asking him about his day. Since Lisa's death he'd gotten into the habit of talking to the dog. Oreo had become his companion so he told her what was on his mind.

"Hope needs a kids' doctor. Jaclyn's clinic is unusable, but Dad's old building might make a good replacement." The dog shifted and he nodded. "I know. It's probably a wreck."

Kent didn't want to admit how much seeing Jaclyn had affected him. He was grateful when a car's lights flashed as it climbed the hill to his ranch house. Company would be good.

He gulped when Jaclyn climbed out of a sky-blue convertible and walked toward him—limped, actually. She had on a pair of jeans, a perfectly pressed candy-pink shirt and a pair of white sneakers that looked brand-new. Typical city girl.

"Hello." Her smile displayed perfect white teeth. Everything about her was perfect.

"Hi." He motioned to a chair. "How's the foot?" he asked when she'd sat.

"Sore." She tucked some of the glossy silver-blond strands behind one ear before she bent to pet his dog. "But fine."

"Good." Suddenly he could think of nothing to say.

"I wanted to thank you again for saving me this afternoon, Kent. I would have died without your help." Her big brown eyes stared earnestly into his.

"Don't thank me." He heard the gruffness in his voice and wished he could sound less affected by her presence. He didn't want her to guess how much seeing her again *had* affected him. "One of the other guys would have found you."

"But you were the one who did and you treated my foot. So thank you." She paused a moment.

"Sure. Anything else?" It was rude and ungracious but

suddenly Kent didn't want to talk to Jaclyn. She upset his carefully regulated world.

"Yes, there is. You mentioned your dad's office building."

"Yeah." He kept it noncommittal.

"I noticed it's unoccupied. Is renting it an option?" Her voice became businesslike.

"I don't know. I haven't been through the place in ages." Why had he ever opened his big mouth? He wanted to avoid her, not build a relationship. When hope flickered in her eyes he blurted out the first excuse he could think of. "There could be some issues with the place."

"Can you check?" Jaclyn rubbed the sweet spot behind Oreo's ears and smiled at the dog's growled appreciation. She refocused on Kent. "It's really important to me to get the clinic going again." Her eyes held his. "Please?"

"I've got the ranch and my practice," he reminded. "I'm pretty busy."

"I'm sure you are." She kept staring, waiting.

"Fine," he relented when it became obvious she wouldn't back off. "I'll look as soon as I can." In the meantime maybe she'd find something else and he could forget her and go on with his normal life.

In his dreams. He remembered Jaclyn's tenacity too well.

"If you'd let me know when you go, I'd like to come along." Her smile blazed. "The clinic has to be fully operational, treating a certain number of patients, in three months or I jeopardize my financing. This is March. That means I'd have to move in by the end of May."

"I said I'll get to it when I can and I will." He swallowed his harsh tone and focused on his manners. She was his guest and he hadn't offered her anything. His mother would be appalled. "Do you want something to drink?"

"Iced tea? If it's not too much trouble."

Kent went inside and reached for the fridge door. To his

shock, Jaclyn followed him and was now looking around the kitchen. He wished he hadn't offered her a drink. Or anything else. He didn't want her here, seeing the starkness of his kitchen and realizing that it mirrored his life. He didn't want her leaving behind the scent of her fancy perfume. Mostly he didn't want her seeing how pathetic he was.

He held out a brimming glass.

"Thanks. Do you have any lemon?" She accompanied the request with the sweetest smile.

Kent hacked off a wedge of lemon and held it out.

"Oh." She took it daintily between her fingertips—perfectly manicured fingertips with pale pink polish. "Um, thank you." She moved to stand in front of the sink, pinched the lemon into her glass and stirred it with a finger. "Lovely." She held the piece of lemon between two fingers, searching for a place to discard it.

Kent handed her a sheet of paper towel.

"Thanks." She wrapped the towel around the lemon wedge and set it on the counter before she took another sip. "It feels cool out tonight."

Meaning he could hardly lead her outside to the patio again. He motioned to one of the kitchen chairs. Jaclyn sank onto it with graceful elegance. Kent couldn't help noticing her expensive jeans, her tailored blouse, and her three pieces of jewelry—two small gold hoops in her ears and a thin gold chair around her neck—that made her look like a princess slumming it.

"Are you still holding that night at the church against me, Kent?"

"What?" He jerked to awareness, embarrassed that he'd been caught staring at her. "Of course not. Why would you say that?"

"You act as if you're mad at me." Her smile grew wistful. "I never came back to Hope for any of the reunions and

I haven't seen you since the night of high school graduation, so I'm guessing your attitude has to be about the night I wrecked the church. I'll apologize again if it means you'll forgive me for letting you take the blame for that night, even for a little while."

Forgive her? He was the one who needed forgiveness. But what he'd done was unforgiveable.

"Am I forgiven?" Her smile faltered.

"Nothing to forgive," Kent told her, his voice hoarse. "You were hurting. Your sister had just died. You were angry that God hadn't healed her the way you expected and you lashed out. I understood."

"You always did." Jaclyn's voice softened to a whisper. "Of all the people in Hope, you were the only one who did. But I shouldn't have let you take the fall, even for the few days it took to get my act together. I'm sorry."

"I'm glad I could help." High-school Jaclyn had drawn his sympathy, but this woman disarmed him. His throat was dry. He took a sip of his tea but it didn't seem to help. Nor did it stop the rush of awareness that she was the first woman to come into Lisa's kitchen since—

"You helped me more than you ever knew. I won't forget that." After an introspective silence her expression changed, her voice lightened. "I don't suppose we could go into town and look at your dad's building tonight? Don't answer. I can see 'no' written all over your face. How about tomorrow morning? Say, seven-thirty?"

"Do you ever give up?" he asked in exasperation.

Jaclyn stilled. "Not when it comes to my dreams."

"This clinic is your dream?" Kent knew it was from the expression on her face. He also knew he wanted to help her achieve it. "I'll ask a friend of mine to check out my dad's old office as soon as he can. But be warned it will probably need a painting, at the very least. The company that opened the new silver mine on the other side of Hope was in there last and they weren't gentle."

"Your dad's retired now, I suppose? He and your mom were such a loving couple. I remember she once told my mom the ranch was your dad's weekend toy but he intended to make it a full-time job after retirement." She tilted her head to one side, studying the fancy kitchen. "Your mom must love this. Everything here looks brand-new."

"It is. My wife had it redone several years ago. My parents died in a car accident, Jaclyn. That's why I came back to Hope." Kent clamped his lips together.

"Oh, no!" She shook her head sadly. "Losing your parents must have been hard."

"Yes, it was."

After a long silence, she asked, "Is your wife here? I'd like to meet her. There aren't a lot of the kids from our class in Hope anymore. Since my parents sold our ranch right after I finished high school, I've kind of lost touch."

Kent stiffened. But he had to tell her. She'd hear it from someone in town anyway. Better that he laid out the bare truth. Maybe when she knew, she'd stay away and let him get back to his solitary life.

"My wife was Lisa Steffens."

"I remember Lisa—"

"She's dead," he blurted out.

"Oh, Kent. I'm so truly sorry."

"She died in a fire. A fire I set." Kent wished he could have avoided rehashing the past.

Jaclyn blinked. She studied him for several moments before she said, "You didn't do it deliberately. I know you and you couldn't have done that."

"You don't know me anymore, Jaclyn."

"I don't think you've become a murderer, Kent." She held his gaze. "Do you mind telling me what happened?"

Jaclyn's presence in his house made the place come alive as it hadn't in a very long time. She brought color to the cold stainless steel, life to the gray tones that only reminded him of death and guilt. From somewhere deep inside a rush of yearning gripped Kent, a yearning to share his life with someone who would talk, listen and laugh with him. If only he could enjoy Jaclyn's company and the hope that was so much a part of her aura—just for a little while.

"Not tonight." He drew back, regrouped.

Once Kent had dreamed of happiness, a family, a future on this ranch. He'd failed Lisa and he'd never have that now. But he had to go on; he couldn't get sidetracked by his crazy attraction to Jaclyn LaForge, no matter how strong. He admired her courage in returning to Hope, in sticking to her promise to her sister, but he desperately needed to resume his carefully structured world because that was the only way he could survive the guilt.

It wasn't his job to get Jaclyn a new clinic. He didn't want to get involved. He didn't want concerns about whether her foot would heal properly or get infected. And he sure didn't want his heart thudding every time he saw her.

Every instinct Kent possessed screamed *Run!*

"I'll meet you at the building tomorrow morning at eight," he heard himself say.

Chapter Two

"This is a beautiful building. The windows give amazing light."

"Say it, Jaclyn. There's a lot of work needed here." Kent leaned against a doorframe, probably running a repair tab in his mind. Then his gaze rested on her.

Jaclyn frowned. Maybe he was waiting for her to say she didn't want to rent his father's building.

"Correction—more than a lot of work." Kent kept staring at her.

"Perhaps once all the borders are removed?" Jaclyn trailed her finger across a wall.

"My mom went a little over the top with the borders," Kent admitted. "She loved the themes and colors of southwest decorating."

His wife definitely hadn't. Jaclyn wondered why Lisa had chosen the gray color scheme for her kitchen. High-tech certainly, but it seemed clinical, with nothing to soften the harsh materials or unwelcoming, austere colors. Her curiosity about Lisa's death had been tweaked by Kent's admission that he set the fire. Jaclyn knew there was no way he'd have deliberately hurt her. Kent had been in love with Lisa since seventh grade.

While Kent became all business, talking about support

beams and studs, her attention got sidetracked as her eyes took in an unforgettable picture. The handsome vet probably couldn't care less what he looked like, but he was without a doubt what Jaclyn's friend Shay would say was hunk material.

A moment later Kent's dark blue gaze met hers and one eyebrow arched.

She'd missed something. Heat burned her cheeks. "Sorry?"

"I said it's going to be a while before you can move in here."

"A while meaning what, exactly?" She hadn't been staring. Well, not intentionally.

Liar.

"Are you okay?" Kent tilted his head to study her. "You look kind of funny."

"I'm fine." Jaclyn cleared her throat. Business. Concentrate on business. "You're telling me there's work that has to be done here, which I know. How long will that take?"

"I can't tell you that." Kent frowned. "Since the mine opened last spring, a lot of locals have gone to work there. The place offers good wages, decent benefits and steady work which means there aren't a lot of qualified trades available in Hope anymore."

"But? I can hear a 'but' in there." She smiled and waited.

"I'll start on the demolition. I can do most of that myself and some of the actual renovation. There are a couple of guys I can probably persuade to do other work but it is going to take time." He looked like he was waiting for her to say "never mind."

But Jaclyn wouldn't say that—getting this clinic operational again was her duty. The clinic had been her dream since the day after she'd buried her twin sister. They both should have graduated from high school but Jessica's diagnosis had come too late, because of the shortage of doctors in Hope. The traveling doctors that visited each week didn't catch the leukemia early enough. That wouldn't happen to another child—not if Jaclyn could help it.

She had already checked the other buildings in town. This place was the best of the lot, but Kent was right. It needed a major overhaul.

"I have just over three months until I have to open. Can you do it?"

He frowned, his deep blue eyes impassive. Only the twitch at the corner of his mouth told her he'd rather be somewhere else. "I *believe* I can."

Relief swamped her, stealing her restraint. She threw her arms around him and hugged.

"Thank you, Kent. Thank you so much."

He froze, his whole body going stiff. After a moment he lifted one hand and awkwardly patted her shoulder before easing away. "I haven't done anything yet."

"I can see it finished." She twirled around, her imagination taking flight. "Reception will be here, of course. I don't remember what your dad had in this corner before, but I'll get a child's table-and-chair set for coloring. And we can put—"

"That was Arvid's corner."

"Arvid?" She stared at Kent as old memories surfaced. "Your dad's parrot!" She grinned. "That's an idea."

"You'd put a parrot in a doctor's office?" His nose wrinkled. "Isn't that against health regulations or something?"

"Not as long as the cage is kept clean and the animal isn't dangerous. It's actually a great idea. I wonder where I'd find a parrot around here."

"At the ranch. I've got Arvid out there, hanging in the sunroom for now. He stays there during winter, but soon I'll have to bring him into the main house so he doesn't get overheated." Kent made a face. "He's never really adapted to the ranch. He doesn't like my dog. Or me," he admitted.

"You're sure it wouldn't be too much for him? Would the kids overwhelm him?"

Kent laughed. She hadn't heard that jubilant sound in years but the pure pleasure filling his face captivated her. In the moment, he looked carefree, happy.

"*Overwhelm* him?" His eyes twinkled. "You must not remember Arvid very well. The only thing that ever overwhelmed that bird was my mother's broom."

She giggled, sharing his mirth. But a moment later Kent's eyes met hers and his smile melted away. In a flash his glowering expression was back.

"You're certain you can get this place ready for me to use in time?" Jaclyn wished she could make his smile appear again. But she reminded herself that she didn't have the time for personal relationships with grumpy vets, not even the ones who made her heart skip a beat.

"I'm not certain but I think so. I spoke to a couple of tradesmen this morning."

"This morning?" *And I thought I got up early.* "And?" she asked.

"They'll stop by later today to take a look. Then I'll have a better idea." He rubbed a hand against his freshly shaven chin. "You understand I can't guarantee anything. At the moment there are just too many unknowns. All I can say is that I'll do my best."

"I understand. Your best is good enough for me."

"I'm not sure you do understand." He tipped her chin so she had to look at him. "Listen to me, Jaclyn. I have my practice and the ranch. I'm the fire chief, the mayor and I sit on several local boards. Right now Hope is a town divided over allowing the mine to open. Some folks saw potential, of course. But a lot thought the mine would bring problems. Which it has. And it's cost us some of the small town security we've always enjoyed. That's just a few of the reasons which caused a big split and left a lot of people hurting. I'm trying to help heal that rift."

"You're saying you will have to juggle a lot and that the clinic isn't necessarily first on the list." She nodded. "I get that and I accept it. I have to. I don't have another option. I have a lot invested in getting this clinic going and I'm willing to do whatever it takes." She caught his skeptical glance at her hands and smiled. "Just because I haven't lived on a ranch for a while doesn't mean I don't know how to work hard."

"Okay then. I'll do the best I can." Kent nodded once.

"And I'll help however I can. Just ask." Her beeper interrupted. Jaclyn glanced at it. "I have to go."

"What will you do for offices in the meantime?" Kent asked.

"The hospital gave me a room to use for consulting, for now. Not that I need much. People here don't seem willing to trust me." She tried to swallow the bitterness.

"Folks in Hope take a while to embrace outsiders." He blinked, obviously only then remembering that she wasn't exactly an outsider. "I had my own struggle after Doc McGregor died. It took forever for people to let me treat their cattle."

"And you weren't even guilty of almost burning down the local church." She grimaced. "Nobody's going to stop seeing me as that stupid kid. Maybe it was dumb of me to think I could come back here."

"No, it wasn't. People here will get to know you. Some will remember you were just a kid who lost your sister. Besides, you and your parents repaired the damage. Not that it matters anyway. The church is in bad condition now."

"Maybe I could find a way to restore it," she murmured. "Maybe that would make them forget."

"It's a nice thought." His tanned brow furrowed. "But it's not just your past. Your family only lived here for a few years, Jaclyn—your parents left when you did and neither they nor you ever came back. I'm not trying to hurt you, but to folks in Hope, you *are* an outsider."

"But I'm trying to help them!"

"I know." Kent nodded. "But while you've been away things have changed. Because of the mine, people here are more suspicious than ever before."

"Is that even possible?" she quipped.

"Oh, yeah." He didn't smile. "I told you the town had split over the mine, but I didn't tell you that the split was caused by outsiders who set friends and neighbors against each other, using scare tactics, among other things. Everyone's suspicious of everyone right now. But folks will come around. We need your clinic, Jaclyn."

We need your clinic? She liked the sound of that.

"Don't give up on your dream, okay?"

"No chance of that—I owe it to Jessica." The beeper sounded again. "Thanks, Kent." Jaclyn waggled her fingers as she strode toward her car.

After she had treated the baby who'd ingested his brother's marble, she sat and enjoyed her first cup of coffee of the day, recalling the note of earnestness in Kent's voice when he'd told her not to give up.

Remembering the forlorn look on his face last night when she'd visited his ranch, she wanted to repeat it back to him.

But now she wondered, what *were* Kent's dreams?

Dr. Jaclyn LaForge possessed remarkable powers of persuasion.

As he watched her drive away, Kent couldn't quite quash his smile. He walked through his dad's building a second time, remembering her insistence that she would help with renovations. As if those manicured hands would know how to grip a hammer.

His smile faded as he noted issues he'd missed. He should have been in here before this.

He should have done a lot of things.

Like not notice how Jaclyn's smile made her eyes as glossy as black walnut fudge. Like escape that hug she'd laid on him. Like ignore the way she'd lured him into helping her reach that goal of hers. The hurt in her eyes when she revealed that she'd been rebuffed by the locals had nearly done him in.

Kent drew on his memories of the LaForge twins. Jessica had always been the serious twin, Jaclyn the prankster. But after her sister's death, Jaclyn had bottled up her pain and anger until she'd finally exploded on graduation night. He'd understood why. Jaclyn had put so much faith in believing God would heal her sister. She couldn't reconcile Jessica's death with that faith. That's why she'd torn up the newly planted flower beds at the church. It was the reason she'd spray painted the walls and made a mess that had scandalized the entire town. Jaclyn had needed answers that night and she hadn't been able to find any that satisfied.

He knew how that felt. He'd asked why so many times. He still didn't have the answer he craved. He wondered if Jaclyn had ever found hers.

Uncomfortable with the direction of his thoughts, Kent reconsidered Jaclyn. She was still stunningly beautiful, but she'd lost the easy, confident joy in life that had once been so much a part of her. Jaclyn now seemed hunted, as if she had to prove something. He recalled her words.

I owe it to Jessica.

Kent knew all about obligations, and about failing them. Boy, did he know. He veered away from the familiar rush of guilt and recalled instead the closeness between the sisters. He, like others in their youth group, had attended many prayer services for Jessica in the small adobe church. But Jessica had died in spite of Jaclyn's insistence that if they just asked heaven enough times, God would respond.

Clearly the obligation to her sister still drove Jaclyn.

Brimming with questions that had no answers, Kent continued his inspection of the building. He pressed the wall in several places where water leaks had soaked through the plaster and left huge spots of dark brown. Each time he pushed, hunks of soggy plaster crumbled and tumbled to the floor. It would all have to be removed.

His former tenants had complained about something in the bathroom. Too busy with Lisa's depression, the failing ranch and his own pathetic practice to tend to the matter himself, Kent had hired a plumber. He now saw that the work was substandard. The bathroom would need to be gutted.

There were other issues, too. The roof, for one. Some of the clay tiles had cracked and broken away. Summer rains in Hope were aptly named monsoons. This past summer, the water had managed to find a way in, ruining large portions of the ceiling.

Kent made four phone calls. Then he took off his jacket, rolled up his shirtsleeves and got to work hauling refuse out to the newly arrived Dumpster he'd ordered. He'd been working about two hours before a phone call sent him back to his clinic at the ranch to treat a family pet. One thing after another popped up until it was evening. He wanted nothing more than to sprawl out in his recliner and relax, but he'd promised Jaclyn that building and her deadline would roll around too soon.

After a quick meal, Kent filled a thermos with coffee, grabbed an orange and headed back into town. At sunset his high school chum Zac Enders stopped in.

"Out for the usual run, huh, Professor?" Kent used the old nickname deliberately because it bugged Zac. He tossed yet another shovel full of plaster into a bin.

"Yeah. What's going on here?" Zac grabbed a push broom and slid a new pile of rubbish onto Kent's shovel. "You sell the place?"

"I wish." Kent dumped the load, stood the shovel and leaned on its handle. "You didn't hear about Jaclyn's clinic burning?"

"Actually I did. I was out of town for a two-day conference but someone at the office filled me in." Zac had become the superintendent of Hope's school district the previous fall. "Shame."

"Yeah, it is." Kent waved a hand. "She wants to use this place. She's got to be up and running within three months." He gave his buddy the short version.

"This time you've really bitten off a big piece, cowboy." Zac smirked when Kent's head shot up at the old moniker. "Aren't high school nicknames fun?"

"Yeah," Kent said with a droll look. "Real fun."

"This place is a disaster." Zac glanced around, his eyes giving away his concern. "I hope you believe in miracles."

Kent didn't believe in miracles. Miracles would have saved his wife from the depression that took hold of her spirit and never let go. Miracles would have made him a better husband, would have helped him know how to help her. Miracles would have saved Lisa from getting caught between a wildfire and the backfire he'd set to stop it.

"I didn't make Jaclyn any promises," he told Zac. "I'll do my best here and hopefully it will be enough. But I don't know what I can do about Jaclyn's other problems." He shook his head at Zac's puzzled look. "Apparently, the good people of Hope are reluctant to go to Jaclyn for medical help."

"Ah. The vandalism is coming back to bite her. But you can change that, Kent."

"Me?"

"Yes, you," Zac shot back. "Everybody in Hope thinks you're God's gift."

Kent snorted. "Hardly." God's failure, maybe.

"It's true. They look to you for leadership and they do whatever you say. All you have to do is put out a good word about her clinic and Jaclyn will have more patients than she can handle. I should know. That's how I got my job."

"Not true. You got your job because you were the best candidate."

"And because you put in a word with the board chairman." Zac smiled. "I heard."

"I only said it would be nice to have someone with a PhD running things." Kent avoided his knowing look.

"So? You can do the same for Jaclyn." Zac paused, frowned. "Can't you?"

"I've already tried. But she's big city now, Zac." Kent stared at the shovel he held. "Designer everything. You know how that goes down in Hope."

"I do know. Everyone still feels conned by the city jerks that came here, promised the moon and have yet to deliver. But so what?" His friend studied him for several moments then barked a laugh. "Surely you can't imagine Jaclyn will leave? Don't you remember high school at all, cowboy?"

"Which part of high school?" Kent remembered some parts too well. Like how he was going to marry Lisa and live happily ever after.

"Dude! The Brat Pack, remember?" Zac nudged him with an elbow. "Jaclyn, Jessica, Brianna and Shay? Their dream?"

"I had forgotten that." Kent recalled the closeness of the four, the way Shay and Brianna had rallied around Jaclyn while her sister suffered. He vaguely remembered the friends discussing some future project they'd all be part of.

"They were going to build a clinic. Then Jessica died. The others decided to make the clinic as a kind of monument to her. They were each going to have a specialty. Jaclyn, the pediatrician who made sure no child ever had the lack of care her sister did, Brianna wanted to practice child psychology and Shay was going to be a physiotherapist." Zac slapped his shoulder. "You've got to put in a good word for Jaclyn, man. She's spent a long time nursing that dream."

"Ah, yes, Brianna." Kent frowned. "You wouldn't still be waiting for your former fiancée to come back to Hope to work in this clinic, would you, Professor?"

"No." Zac shook his head, his eyes sad. "I gave up that dream long ago when I heard Brianna had married."

"Then what's your interest?" Kent raised his shoulders.

"I live here. I knew and liked Jessica. I think it would be cool if Jaclyn finally got to make her dream come true and cooler still if you helped her do it. But that's up to you." He looked around, flexed his arm. "Want a hand? I haven't got anything going on tonight."

"Great. You're better at cleaning than me," Kent teased.

"If you consider this place clean, then I certainly am." Zac and Kent worked as a team for several hours. As usual, Zac brought the conversation around to discussing his first love—Hope's schools. "Are you listening to me?" he asked.

"Sure." Kent blinked, grinned. "Not really."

"Thinking about Jaclyn, huh?" Zac snickered. "I hear she's changed."

"I told you, she's turned big city." Kent shrugged.

"That doesn't mean she's different inside." Zac drank from his water bottle while Kent sipped his coffee. "She's still focused on that clinic."

"I'd substitute 'driven' for 'focused.'" Kent sat on an upturned pail. "It's like the clinic will happen or she'll die trying."

"What's wrong with that?" Zac asked.

"Lots." Kent waved a hand around them. "What's going to

happen if I don't get finished in time? She'll lose her funding. But Jaclyn doesn't hear my warnings and, far as I can tell, she doesn't have an alternate plan. It's the clinic or nothing."

"So you finish this place." Zac blinked. "What's the problem?"

"The problem?" Kent made a face. "Oh, just a few insignificant issues, like finding someone to do the work, paying for it, spending time here that I should be spending on my own practice or the ranch—take your pick." Suddenly the magnitude of what he'd agreed to swamped him. "I don't want to be responsible for ruining her dream."

"Her dream? Or Lisa's?" Zac tilted his head to one side, his expression sober. "It wasn't your fault Lisa didn't get her dream."

"Yes, it was. I'm the one who dragged her away from the city. I'm the one who wouldn't leave the ranch when she asked me to." The guilt multiplied every time Kent thought about his actions. He'd loved Lisa yet he'd hurt her deeply.

"How could you have walked away from the ranch?" Zac asked quietly. "You would have lost everything. That's not what a responsible man does."

"Not even at the cost of his wife's happiness?" Kent growled.

"There's no evidence that moving would have guaranteed happiness. Lisa was sick. You told me the doctors said moving would change nothing."

"They said it, but I don't *know* that. Maybe if I'd forced her into treatment—"

"You can't force someone to be well, Kent," Zac said, his voice somber. "You did what you could."

But Kent knew he hadn't done enough. He'd tried to force Lisa to see the good things about living on the ranch, but all she saw was a trap that kept her from the fairy tale dream in her mind of a happy, party-style life in the city.

Zac helped awhile longer then offered some advice before he left.

"Lisa's gone. Leave her with God. He knows you did your best. He loves you and understands. Move on."

God loved him?

After Zac left, Kent tidied up the place, gathered his thermos and shut off the lights while thinking about Zac's words. Kent felt he couldn't accept God's love because he wasn't worthy of it. Lisa would still be alive if not for him. So what if they'd lost the ranch? He'd persisted because he wanted to make his dad's dream for the place come alive when he should have let it go and started again.

Shoulda, woulda, coulda.

The awful truth was that he'd chosen his father's dream over his wife.

Kent wouldn't make that mistake again. Somehow he'd get this building ready for Jaclyn, no matter what it cost him. It couldn't bring Lisa back or erase his guilt over her death, but maybe it would ease Jaclyn's grief.

He had to remember only one thing.

No matter how beautiful or how interesting Jaclyn was, no matter how many times he felt that zing of attraction when she smiled at him, there could be nothing between them.

Kent's love had failed the one woman he'd pledged to cherish. That would not happen again because as far as he was concerned, he had nothing to offer a woman but failure.

Jaclyn was a friend, but that's all she could ever be.

Chapter Three

"I'm begging, Pete. I know you're full-time at the mine, but I just need a couple of hours of your time. That's all."

Jaclyn paused in the doorway, struck by Kent's tone. Were plumbers so hard to get? She hadn't considered that. She'd figured Kent would pick up the phone, hire someone to do the renovation and she'd move in. But he sounded almost desperate.

"I didn't realize you had an exclusivity clause. Maybe if you asked them to waive it, they'd let you help with the clinic. It's for a good purpose, for our town's benefit. That's what their people promised when they begged us to let the mine in." He paused for effect. "This would be a good opportunity to keep that promise." There was silence as he listened. "I really appreciate it, Pete. Thanks."

Not wanting to be caught eavesdropping, Jaclyn waited a few moments before she let the front door bang behind her. "Hello?"

"Hi." Kent blinked at her. He was covered in a chalky dust that turned his dark hair gray. He'd been putting on goggles but now pulled them away, his blue eyes meeting hers. "Are you slumming?"

"Pretty fancy slum you've got here," she teased.

"Not yet, but it will be if I can get it done." He frowned. "Did you need something?"

"No. But I thought you might. I came to see if there was something I could help you with this evening." Jaclyn made a face. "Emergency was busy today—an issue with the mine. I need to work off the stress. I figured if you were into demolition, I'd channel my energy into that. Have you eaten dinner?" She glanced around amazed by the mess he'd created.

"I haven't had time for dinner." Kent gave her pristine clothes a dark look. "You can't work here dressed like that. Leave this to me, Jaclyn."

"Nonsense. I make a perfectly good gofer assistant and I can clean with the best of them. Besides, I've got the clothes issue covered. But first we eat. Deal?" She waited for his nod before setting down the two bags she'd carried in. She removed containers of Chinese food from one. "Come on. Let's sample this while it's hot."

At first it seemed as if Kent would refuse. Maybe he was used to working alone, or maybe he thought she'd get in his way. Either way Jaclyn wasn't going to let it dissuade her from pitching in.

"Thank you," he said when she handed him a loaded plate of stir fried vegetables.

"Welcome." She separated her chopsticks then speared a piece of pineapple. "Yum."

"It is good. Thanks," he said again, looking directly at her, his blue eyes bright.

"I don't know if Chinese is rancher's food but nobody in town has takeout steaks." She giggled at his droll look. "I'm guessing by that kitchen of yours that Lisa was a gourmet cook."

Kent's hand froze halfway to his mouth, his face pale at the mention of his wife.

"I'm so sorry," she said, feeling a fool. "I didn't mean to bring back painful memories."

"No, it's okay." He inhaled slowly then let out his pent-up breath before he spoke. "Lisa liked to cook if it was for entertaining—invite people over and she would go all out."

"I remember some parties Lisa invited me to in high school. She was a fantastic hostess back then, and an amazing cook." She watched the sadness of his face ease. "I suppose entertaining does provide an incentive to create. Not that I'd know. I can do basic cooking, which means I can open soup cans." Jaclyn took a bite, waiting to see if Kent would continue talking about Lisa or if he would change the subject.

"What happened at the mine?" he asked. "Anything serious?"

Note to self, she thought: *stop bringing up Lisa.*

"A chemical explosion left burns on a number of miners. Emergency was swamped. This isn't the day for the traveling doctors so the hospital asked me to help. There were no critical injuries, so that's a blessing." She shuddered. "I loathe treating burns."

"Why?" Kent studied her with a puzzled look.

"Because of the pain. Kids or adults, it doesn't matter. Burns are the worst for continued pain. After initial treatment there's always the task of debrading the scar tissue to allow new tissue to grow—very time-consuming and more pain for the patient." She blinked. "As a firefighter, you probably know that."

"Since I've been on the job we've never had anyone badly burned, thank heaven." Kent said.

"That's lucky. Now—" Jaclyn lifted out a surprise "—I scored this from the bakery. Are you interested?"

"Who wouldn't be interested in key lime pie?" Kent raised an eyebrow when she cut a slice.

"What?" She studied the piece then chuckled. "Too small?

Well, okay then." Jaclyn whacked out a much larger hunk of pie with her plastic knife. "Better?"

"Much better. Thank you." He dug in with relish.

"I'll have to jog for hours after this." She tasted her pie and sighed.

"You can join Zac. He's always jogging." Kent told her about their other school friend, Nick, and she shared the latest on her best friends Shay and Brianna.

"I remember Shay was offered some kind of contract just after her dad lost his job," Kent said.

"Modeling, yes. She felt she couldn't decline it because they needed the money so badly. Her father was broke. But he's gone now and she's finishing her physiotherapy degree. And Brianna is a practicing psychologist now in Chicago."

Kent finished his pie and added the plate and plastic fork to his garbage load.

"Both Shay and Brianna have gone through tough times." Jaclyn gnawed on her lower lip. "It's difficult to understand why things happen. Sometimes it seems to me that God expects too much of us humans."

"I'll second that." The words spilled out of Kent in a rush of bitterness.

"I'm sure you miss Lisa," she said before she could stop herself. So much for not bringing her up.

He nodded, accepted the cup of coffee she offered and they drank in silence for a while.

"I'm on call tonight so I might have to take off at any moment. We'd better get to work." She cleaned up the remains from their meal then met his gaze. "What can I do to help?"

"It's not necessary, really, Jaclyn." Kent glanced at her clothes again then quickly busied himself donning his mask and gloves. "The meal was more than enough."

Jaclyn let him go back to work then put on the white paper coveralls she'd brought, along with gloves and a mask. She began tapping the wall, trying to imitate Kent's motions on the plaster surface. She must have tapped too hard because huge chunks dropped down at her feet.

"I'm not sure I need this much help," he said, blue eyes twinkling.

"So tell me what I can do to help because I'm not going away." She met his stare head-on, relieved when he finally gave a half nod.

"How about stripping the wallpaper?"

"I can do that." She followed his directions and for the next hour worked feverishly, spraying, scrubbing and peeling away the old borders as she forced the stress from her mind and her muscles.

"How's work going? Are you swamped yet?" Kent steadily removed the damaged material from the walls, never missing a stroke as he spoke.

"Ha! I wish. My practice is on the way to failure. People won't even look me in the eye when I meet them on the street. Especially since I asked about the church and how it could be restored." She yanked extra hard on a strip of paper and smiled as the entire piece came loose. "At last."

He shrugged. "It might take a while but you'll break through their reserve."

"When will that be?" she demanded. "The day after the clinic closes because I don't have any patients?"

"It's not that bad," he muttered.

"You think not? A woman came into the hospital with a sick baby today. I tried to help, but the mom took the kid away, saying they'd drive to Las Cruces. You know how far that is, especially for a sick child?" Frustration leached through though she tried to suppress it. "If this continues, it won't matter if I open this clinic or not." She gulped down her panic. "I need patients, Kent."

He put down his hammer and turned to her.

"I'm really sorry this is happening, Jaclyn. It must feel terrible to be treated like that when you're just trying to help."

"I don't care about me," she sputtered. "It's the kids that matter. Their parents won't let me help."

"None of them?" His voice softened, flowing over her with compassion.

"Not many. Officially I have eleven juvenile patients on my books. Eleven, Kent, in a population of—what's the population of Hope? Three thousand?" She clenched her left hand as tears welled in spite of her efforts to suppress them. "I came here because I'm trying to make sure no other kid gets missed like Jessica did. Why is that wrong?"

"It's not wrong." He rested a comforting hand on her shoulder. "It's a wonderful, unselfish, kind and generous thing to do."

"It can't be that wonderful." She dashed the tears away. "I know that God has a purpose for each of our lives, something only we can accomplish for him. I believe the clinic is my purpose. I've been praying about it for years. I'm here. I'm ready. So why doesn't God help?"

If only Kent McCloy were privy to God's thoughts.

"I don't think I can explain God's actions." Kent lifted his hand off her delicate shoulder and turned so she couldn't see his face. "I think I'm on a need-to-know basis with heaven."

"Because of Lisa's death, you mean?" Jaclyn sat down on an old sawhorse he'd brought from home, watching him carefully, her big brown eyes inviting him to share. "I can't even imagine how hard it must have been for you. Do you want to talk about it?"

Hard didn't begin to describe it, but no matter the release he might find sharing with Jaclyn, Kent wasn't going to do it. He knew he was to blame. He didn't want to watch the pity fill her eyes.

"No, I don't." That came off sounding harsh so he changed the subject back to her. "Eventually people will get to know you and realize your heart is right." The last thing Hope needed was to lose yet another doctor. "Don't give up."

"Oh, I'm frustrated, Kent. But I'm a long way from giving up." She rose, took another swipe at the wallpaper. "So how do I go about getting to know the people of Hope?"

"I'm not sure." He carried a bucket of refuse out to the Dumpster. When he returned, Jaclyn was grinning. "What?"

"I have a great idea. I'm going to join some of their local groups. I can't cook and I haven't got a clue how to quilt, but if those groups exist here, I'll join them." Her chin lifted in determination. "You'll have to tell me what kind of activities Hope offers because this place isn't at all as I remember."

"It's the same place, but we've gone through some issues. When the town split over the mine almost two years ago, there were a lot of hard feelings. Cliques developed." She frowned at him and he sought an example to illustrate his point. "Like there used to be a ladies' aid society, but it's for the pro ladies now," he told her. "Pro meaning pro-mine. The ladies against the mine and the problems they thought it would bring to their families left that group and started their own. That one is called Hope Circle and it has no relationship with the other group."

"Should I join one, or both?" She frowned, rubbing her chin.

"Don't ask me. I don't even know what they do in their meetings." Kent shrugged. "I only know they do not do it together. We used to have a family bowling night. Everyone came out, brought their kids and had a great time together. Now we have the Christian night and the Followers' night."

"You're kidding me," Jaclyn said with a wry smile. Despite her messy work, she still looked as if she'd stepped out of a magazine. Her white paper suit did nothing to disguise her beauty.

"I wish I were kidding." Kent forced his gaze off her. "The rift goes a lot deeper. Neighbors don't talk to neighbors. Old friends don't have coffee together. Fellow citizens bicker over fence lines and every other petty issue. It's bad. They even insist on different services at the church. The place needs repair badly but nobody is willing to work with anybody else on it." Talking about this made him feel worn-out. "I was a town councilor when it happened. Now I'm the mayor. It's my fault things got so bad."

"You feel responsible?" Jaclyn blinked at him. "Why?"

"I couldn't find a way to mediate, to bring them together." Painful reminders of arguments he'd interrupted, friends he'd tried to reunite and the bitterness underlying everything weighed on his soul. "In the end the town voted on it, the majority won and the mine went ahead, but the issues remain."

"Democracy worked. How is that your fault?" When he stored his hammer in his toolkit, Jaclyn asked, "We're finished for tonight?"

"I am. I'm beat. I had a very early morning." Kent turned away as she shed her paper suit.

There was so much about this woman that spoke to him. Her beauty, her determination to give, her spunky grit in coming here to help him and her strength of purpose in keeping the vow she'd made her sister all demonstrated a woman filled with resolve and fortitude. Her determination astounded him—joining town groups after being virtually ostracized by the community was a gutsy move.

This was one amazing woman.

"There's a long way to go with this place, isn't there?" Her voice was quiet, almost solemn. She stood, holding the leftover pie, waiting for his answer as he locked the building.

"It'll be tough, but it can be done." Kent hoped he wasn't going to regret saying that.

"But it's costing you a lot. I should have considered that." Under the streetlight, Jaclyn's pale hair glowed like a halo around her heart-shaped face. "If you want to back out, tell me. I can find another way."

"Can you?" Kent doubted it.

She looked so small, so delicate. A sudden urge to protect her from the gossip and the hurt she might endure overwhelmed him. Silly. He barely knew Jaclyn anymore.

And yet Kent did know her. He knew her heart was for her patients. He knew her commitment was total. After tonight he also knew her resolve was firm.

"I shouldn't have asked you to do it. You have enough on your plate." A tight little smile curved her very kissable mouth. "I don't want to add to your burdens, Kent."

"Too late." He grinned. "I want to make this clinic happen, Jaclyn." In that moment he realized it was true. "If they could forget their differences, the pristine countryside they've lost, the promises made and broken, the hurt feelings because they didn't see things the same way—if they could only see that their differences are making us all weaker—" He sighed. "Maybe if they could unite in your clinic's cause—well, I guess I see it as a sort of rallying point for people in Hope."

"You do?" A fan of tiny smile lines appeared at the edge of her shining eyes. "How?"

"Your clinic isn't part of the old system. It's new, different. Maybe it can help undo past damage and end some of the bitterness. Maybe that's God's plan in all of this." Kent had no business saying that since he wasn't in touch with God anymore. But his idea about the clinic felt right.

"Thank you for saying that, Kent. I admit I was a little discouraged when I came here tonight, but I feel reenergized now. You can't know how much that means to me." She stood on tiptoe and brushed her lips against his cheek before shoving the pie at him. "You're a wonderful man, Kent. Lisa would be proud of you. Good night." Jaclyn got into her car and drove away.

Lisa would be proud of you.

The surge of hope Kent had experienced drained away. Lisa wouldn't be proud. She would know he was trying to make up for past mistakes. She would recognize that he was trying to redeem himself by getting this clinic up and running.

As if you could redeem yourself for causing your wife's death.

God has a purpose for each of our lives, something only we can accomplish for him. The clinic is my purpose. Jaclyn's words echoed inside his head as he drove the familiar route home.

What's my purpose, God?

But as he pulled up to his house, memories of the past crowded out whatever answers God might have whispered.

If only Kent could have a chance to start fresh, like Jaclyn. He'd do so many things differently.

Maybe if he worked hard enough on her clinic, he could finally rise above his regrets.

Chapter Four

"**B**ut Dr. LaForge is a member of our group."

"She can't be! She's a member of ours."

Two days later the presidents of Hope's two women's committees glared at each other on Main Street—because of her. Jaclyn gulped. What had she gotten into?

"Can't I be a member of both groups?" She heard the timidity in her own voice. Two heads swiveled to stare at her.

"Pro ladies have no relationship with Hope Circle. We stand for different things." Heddy Grange's rigid shoulders tightened even more.

Jaclyn swallowed hard and searched for some middle ground.

"But at the last meeting you discussed doing something to start restoration on the church. Hope Circle is also going to initiate fundraising for that." The moment the words left her lips, Jaclyn knew it was the wrong thing to say.

"You copied our project?" Heddy's voice rose with every word. "How dare you?"

"How dare you?" Missy Sprat snapped back. "We chose it first."

"No, you didn't."

"Ladies, please. Does it matter that you have both cho-

sen to help the place where we all go to meet God?" Jaclyn
thought the role of peacemaker ill-suited to her, but in this
instance she had little choice. This was her fault. "Aren't both
of your groups really trying to extend God's love? Can't that
be done better by working together? Won't He bless all efforts to restore His house?"

The two frowned at her. Their silence lasted only a few
seconds before the wrangling began again. Jaclyn laid a hand
on each arm.

"I'm sorry, ladies. Perhaps it's better if I resign from your
groups," she told them in a no-nonsense tone. "The church is
an important part of my faith which is why I wanted to help
restore it. I never meant to cause problems between you. I
apologize." Then she turned and walked down the street,
aware the women were staring at her retreating back.

"Trouble?" Kent stood in front of his father's building clad
in jeans and a faded chambray shirt. His blue gaze hid behind sunglasses. "The three of you don't look very happy—
you least of all, Doc."

"Happy? No, that would not apply to me at this precise
moment in time." Jaclyn grabbed his arm and pulled him forward. "Please, can we go inside?"

"Need to escape, huh?" His rumbling chuckle shook his
shoulders as he unlocked the door. "As mayor, I've come to
know that feeling very well."

"Why didn't you warn me about what I was walking into?"
Jaclyn flopped down on the sawhorse and exhaled. "I've probably ruined any church restoration plans."

"I doubt it." He chuckled and shook his head. "Those two
were vying for supremacy long before you showed up in
Hope. I don't think your presence here has changed much."

But Jaclyn couldn't laugh. She'd added to the friction in
town and she felt awful. "I should have minded my own
business."

"What happened?" he asked. Before she could finish her explanation he burst out laughing.

"This is not a laughing matter!" She glared at him.

"Sometimes you have to laugh. Or cry at the stupidity of it all." His smile disappeared. "It really isn't your fault. They would have found something to argue about. That's how stupid this quarrel is."

"But I want to be part of the town. That's why I joined those groups, to work toward a common goal. I had this dumb idea that maybe I could make up for the past." She bit her lip. "Instead, I've probably alienated them so much they'll never speak to each other."

"Oh, they'll speak to each other. Otherwise holding the grudge would be pointless." He smiled at her. "Forget about it. You tried to help. Let it go."

"I can't. Somehow I've got to do something to restore that church. If I can do that, maybe the town will find healing there." She blinked, suddenly noticing the floor. "What happened?"

"Mildew. I had to tear out the carpet. Then I found some of the floor boards damaged. The roof leaked during the summer." He scuffed his cowboy boot against a newly installed sheet of plywood. "Renovating this place is like removing an old woman's makeup. You just keep pulling away layers."

"I'm not sure I like the allusion." She frowned. "Why do men always use women as their scapegoats? Cars are 'she.' Fires are 'she.'" Jaclyn saw his shoulders shake with laughter and sighed. "Now I'm bickering! It's contagious."

"Yep. That's why I say forget it. It can get you down if you let it." Kent pulled off his sunglasses and studied her. "We can't afford to lose you, or let you get caught up in somebody else's feud. You've got things to do in Hope, remember?"

And suddenly she did remember. "Oh, brother, now I've done it."

"What?" After a moment he stopped and leaned nearer. "You look funny."

"I feel sick." She slid off the sawhorse onto an upended pail. "How could I be so stupid?"

"What?"

"Kent, I promised I'd speak at those ladies' groups." She watched his smile die.

"What, both of them?"

She nodded. "Separately, of course."

"Well, in light of today's argument, maybe they'll cancel and find somebody else," he offered.

"By tonight?" She shook her head. "Heddy told me how hard it's been to get speakers. Hope isn't exactly sitting in the mainstream of a speaking route. She seemed to like my fundraising ideas and wanted me to tell the Pros about them. Truthfully I was kind of looking forward to it, too. I thought it would make things easier if I provided a little history about my night of terror." She groaned. "Why didn't I shut my mouth? Why did I even try?"

"Because you are generous and trying to help. Relax." Kent pulled out his cell phone and dialed. "Hey, Margie. This is the mayor." He listened for a minute, laughed and then said, "Is there a ladies' group meeting tonight?" His blue eyes twinkled as he listened to the response. "Okay. Sounds like a good time. Thanks." He flipped the phone closed. "It's on and so are you. Apparently the word has gone out about your fundraising ideas for the church and a fair crowd is expected. Margie said she just talked to Heddy and nothing's been canceled, not tonight and not tomorrow night."

"I guess I'll show up then." Jaclyn got hung up on the dimple that sometimes appeared when his eyes crinkled with laughter. "Thanks, Kent. I hope you'll pray for me while I'm there. It's funny but walking into the church's basement makes me feel like Daniel going into the lions' den."

He chuckled but he didn't say he'd pray.

She checked her watch. "Yikes! I've got an appointment. I have to go."

"So I guess that means you won't be by tonight to work," he teased before she dragged open the door.

"I'll stop in and give you the gory details after," she promised. "I'll help you, too, if you want. I have a hunch I'm going to need a good workout before the evening is over."

"Positive thoughts," he ordered.

"I'm positive I was an idiot to even consider this. Nobody can say Hope is boring." She stepped outside to the musical sound of his laughter echoing through the building.

Jaclyn consulted on two cases that afternoon. It felt good to be needed. Later she hurried back to her town home to prepare shrimp salad for the potluck dinner before the meeting. The recipe was Shay's. If it got any accolades tonight, that would be enough. Tiny steps, she reminded herself.

She took her time getting dressed, striving for professional yet not stuffy. The chocolate-brown pencil skirt coordinated perfectly with the pinstriped white-and-brown shirt, and her dark brown heels encased her healing foot like a velvet glove.

"Okay, Lord. That's the best I can do with what you gave me. From here on in it's up to you." The phone rang. "Hi, Mom. How are you?"

Jaclyn winced as her mother launched into a tirade about her father. She suggested her mother discuss it with him.

"He's never here. Golf and more golf. That's his true love."

"Mom, I'm sure Dad loves you as much as he ever did."

Her mother scoffed at that. Clearly her parents' rocky relationship was not improving. In fact it had gone steadily down since the day of Jessica's funeral.

"I found a new site for my clinic," she said, hoping for a diversion.

"When will you give up that silly idea, Jaclyn? You're

our only daughter. You should be here, near us, in a profitable practice."

"Mom, I promised Jess. I have to do this." It was always the same argument and tonight Jaclyn didn't want to get into it. "I'm the speaker at a ladies' meeting in a few minutes. I have to go. I'll call you later," she promised and hung up quickly.

The church parking lot held at least fifty cars. The white stucco church, cornerstone of her childhood and teenage faith, now showed its age. The exterior needed a new coat of paint and repairs on the corners, as did the crumbling stairs. The few undamaged stained windows were cloudy with dust and grime. It looked like birds had taken over the bell tower, and the rosebushes Jaclyn had helped her mom plant as repayment for her vandalism badly needed tending. The carved wooden door she'd ruined ten years ago had been repaired, but it still looked sad and uninspiring. A frisson of despair rippled through her as she saw the gouges she'd made that night. No wonder people hadn't forgotten her vandalism.

But inside Jaclyn was amazed at the transformation of the tired old basement, thanks to candles and some beautiful spring flowers in the center of each table.

Someone took Jaclyn's salad. A moment later Heddy appeared. The woman's beaming face showed no sign of their previous altercation.

"I'm glad you're finally here. I'll introduce you to some members who weren't at our last meeting."

Jaclyn knew she'd never remember all the names so she concentrated on learning about interests and ended up agreeing to take a couple of classes. It was a relief to finally sit down to dinner.

Jaclyn had never tasted anything as delicious as that potluck dinner. She spared a thought for Kent slaving away at her clinic—maybe she'd ask for a plate for him. Before she knew it, Heddy's introduction was over. Jaclyn stood, her knees quaking at the expectant looks.

Please don't let me mess this up. Let me be a help to this hurting community.

Jaclyn started at the beginning, emphasizing God's role in her life and the pain of her twin's death despite so many prayers. She admitted she'd done a lot of damage at the church that night and how sorry she was for it. Then she focused on her reason for returning to Hope.

"I want to be more than just your children's doctor though," she said. "I want to give back to the community." She laid out her ideas for restoring the church. By the time she finished Jaclyn felt she had the sympathy of those listening, but whether or not they'd accept her wasn't clear.

"It's hard to know if I reached them," she told Kent later as he sampled the food she'd brought. "They smiled, thanked me and wished me well, but nobody said they'd bring their kids to see me."

"Give it time." He paused and watched her as she looked around the room. "Well? What do you think of the place now?"

Jaclyn wasn't exactly sure what he expected her to say. She couldn't see any real difference in the room, except that he'd hauled out more garbage. So she simply smiled and said, "Looking good."

"You don't see it, do you?" He shook his head. "No reason why you should, I guess."

Jaclyn tracked his gaze to the window, studied it for several moments.

"I put in a new one," Kent explained. "Zac helped me. He's working out back."

Jaclyn inspected it. "It looks exactly the same," she mused. "You can't tell it's been altered at all."

"That's what I wanted to hear." He grinned. "My dad was

big on southwest architecture so I'm trying to preserve the integrity of the structure."

"He'd be very proud of your work here, Kent." She thought about the ranch. "He must have had plans for the ranch, too."

"Some." Kent's face closed up. He quickly finished his meal and tossed the plate and plastic utensils into the garbage. "That was delicious. It seems like you're always feeding me. It's my turn next time."

"Okay." She smiled at the prospect of sharing another meal with him, until her brain kicked in a reminder that she wasn't here to enjoy Kent McCloy. She was here to keep her promise to Jessica. "Anything I can do to help?"

He looked at her, moving his gaze from her head to her toes. "Um, I don't think so. Not dressed like that. Besides, you'd wreck your nails and muss your hair."

"You're always commenting on my appearance." Jaclyn frowned.

"I don't comment on your appearance all the time. Do I?" He lifted one eyebrow as if he found her comments surprising. "I don't mean to. It's just—"

Jaclyn waited for Kent to complete his thought but when he didn't, she finished it for him.

"Just that I look out of place, like I don't belong here?" She stuffed down the hurt.

"I never said that."

"You didn't have to." She straightened her shoulders and looked directly into his vivid blue eyes. "It's sort of reverse prejudice, isn't it? But I can't do much about it. I look the way I look. I wear the clothes I have. I am who I am. You and everyone else are just going to have to accept that. Or not. Your choice."

"Jaclyn—"

"Good night, Kent." She turned and walked out the door,

surprised by the sting of betrayal. She didn't care what Kent McCloy thought of her.

You just keep telling yourself that, said a voice in her head.

"You're an idiot, cowboy." Zac emerged from the back room wearing a grim expression. "I can't believe you just did that."

"Did what?" Kent muttered.

"Jaclyn offered to help and you shoved it back in her face."

"Did you see what she had on?" he bellowed. "I can hardly ask her to start sanding the wall compound in high heels, can I?"

"Not the point and you know it." Zac's harsh voice left no room for excuses. "You're cranky with me and that's fine. I'm used to your orneriness, but I don't think Jaclyn deserves it. She's only trying to help."

"In those clothes?"

"Oh, get a grip! As if she couldn't have gone home and changed. All she wanted was a chance. But you can't see past her appearance to the heart of her. I never thought you'd be so self-centered, Kent—that you of all people couldn't see past your own biases." Zac dropped the tool bag he was carrying.

Kent didn't know how to answer. But his brain mulled over Zac's words.

"Pete gave me that tool bag. He said he'd be around to-morrow morning and he'd need it then. I have to get home." Zac walked toward the door.

"Professor?" Kent waited for him to turn around. "Thanks for your help."

"No problem. But can I offer some advice?" Zac didn't wait for an invitation. "When you get home tonight, take a look in the mirror and tell me if you're any different from the rest of the naysayers in this town who've already judged our new pediatrician."

"I haven't judged her." Kent ground his teeth at the accusation.

Zac scoffed. "Forget Jaclyn's clothes, her hair and her mannerisms. Jaclyn isn't Lisa, Kent. When you accept that, maybe you'll begin to see past Jaclyn's exterior."

A moment later Zac disappeared, leaving Kent gaping. His best friend had just called him biased. Was that true?

Kent replayed his words to Jaclyn as best he could remember them. He'd said nothing wrong. Except that expression in her eyes—he couldn't get that sad look out of his mind. Like a wounded puppy that expected better of you and was utterly disappointed when you didn't meet her hopes.

Zac was right about that. But he was right about something else, too. Something that was hard for Kent to accept.

Jaclyn did remind him of Lisa.

The two women were nothing alike and yet every time he looked at Jaclyn he saw her clothes, her hairstyle, her fancy shoes—and all of it reminded him of how much Lisa had wanted all those things, and how she'd never gotten them because they'd moved to the ranch.

His phone broke through his musings.

"Hello?" He almost groaned aloud when Heddy, the town's biggest troublemaker, began speaking.

"Thank you for suggesting we ask Dr. LaForge to speak to us, Kent. Some of us remember the damage she did to the church. It's hard to forget. But tonight we realized how much she regrets her past actions. I think we are all impressed by her commitment to reopen the clinic after the fire. According to her, you are the reason she can do that." Heddy paused for breath.

"I'm happy to help." Kent rushed to get a word in before she took off on a new tangent. "I think her ideas to fix the church are amazing, though it's going to take all of us pitching in to make that and her clinic a success." Was that a broad enough hint? Just in case it wasn't, he added, "It takes a lot of patients to make a clinic like hers successful."

"I'm sure it does." Heddy was backing off—he could hear it in her voice. "Of course, I have my own doctor in Las Cruces and anyway, Dr. LaForge is a children's doctor, but I'm sure she's very good at it."

"She certainly comes with high references." Kent paused. He decided to enlighten her, knowing it would flash through the town like wildfire. "She had offers from six other communities, but she chose to set up her practice in Hope."

"Is that right?" Heddy sounded surprised.

"Yes, it is." He paused a moment then added, "I hope we won't make her regret that choice."

"Oh, Kent, dear. Don't worry. There are other doctors to be had." Heddy's breezy, know-it-all tone glossed everything over.

"Then why aren't they here?" Kent saw red at her easy dismissal of the generous doctor who'd slaved night and day trying to give to this town. "Where have they been for the last umpteen years? We need Jaclyn in Hope, Heddy. I would think everyone here could see that after the trouble we've had keeping the hospital functioning."

"Are you getting a little too personally involved, Kent?" The snide undertone irritated.

"I am personally involved," he shot back. "So are you. So is everyone in Hope. Jaclyn lost her sister because of inadequate medical care in this town, and yet she's put away her sorrow so she could come back to help us. I hope we won't be responsible for driving her away because we can't forgive a teenager's mistake. I think we've all made blunders we need forgiveness for. All of us." He paused a moment, added a good-night and hung up. Let Heddy think on that for a while.

But as Kent cleaned up the job site and drove home, his brain kept replaying Jaclyn's face just before she'd left. She reminded him of Lisa when he'd told her he wouldn't move off the ranch. Worse, she reminded him of Lisa's condemnation.

"You hurt people, Kent, because you close yourself off. You won't let anyone, even me, see the vulnerable part of you. What are you so afraid of?"

Once, a long time ago, Jaclyn had asked him exactly the same thing.

He'd been on his way home from dropping off Lisa after the graduation celebration when he'd seen a figure in pale yellow in front of the church.

"Jaclyn?" Kent barely recognized her in the ragged and torn dress. Her eyes were bloodshot and black-ringed from tears that streaked mascara down her cheeks. Then he saw the chaos she'd created. "What are you doing?"

"He's God, isn't He?" Jaclyn sprayed another red jagged line on the white adobe wall of their church, her brown eyes seething with fury. "He wouldn't help Jessica, but He should be able to repair His own church, don't you think? God. The great One. He's supposed to fix everything. Isn't that what they taught us here, Kent?"

"Stop it." He wrenched the paint can out of her hand. "This won't bring Jessica back."

"No, it won't. Nothing will." Jaclyn picked up a stone and hurled it, shattering the small stained-glass window of the youth room. She tore plants from the flower bed and tossed them on the pavement, ignoring the cactus barbs that tore her delicate skin.

"Jaclyn, stop." He'd grabbed her hands, held them in his. "Just stop."

"Stop what—hurting? Stop feeling like God abandoned me, left me hanging when I needed Him most? I wish I could." Her chin thrust forward, her jaw tightened. "Jess should have been there tonight, Kent. She should have been the valedictorian, not me. She should have worn the dress we chose last winter. Why wasn't she?" Fury vibrated in that question. "Because He sat there and did nothing. God let her die."

A second later she'd yanked her hands free and raced to the front door. After removing her shoes, she started hitting the wooden doors with them, antique doors that had guarded entry to the church for almost a century. The gouges from her pointed heels went deep.

"Jaclyn, stop it!" He'd grabbed her arm, tried to drag her away. But anger made her strong. She wrenched free, grabbed the spray can he'd stuck in his pocket and continued her vandalism. Kent tried to stop her but she kept evading him. At last he grabbed her hand and pulled.

"We have to get out of here," he urged when she didn't move.

"Why? What are you afraid of, Kent? That your reputation will be shot 'cause you're here with me? That people will find out you're not the Goody Two-shoes you pretend to be?" She laughed. "Or are you afraid they'll figure out you're not the good little Christian boy they think?"

Kent remembered flashing police lights strobing across her face and the way Jaclyn had pushed against him, hard. She'd dropped the spray can by his feet and run off, her shriek of laughter ending in a muffled sob. He'd stood dumbfounded while the police jumped out of their cars and arrested him.

Oreo drew Kent back to reality, shoving her head against his hand. He'd never forgotten Jaclyn's words. Never stopped wondering how Jaclyn had seen past his carefree facade to his ever-present fear that he failed his parents.

Kent wondered if Jaclyn knew that even after all these years, the fear was still there.

Chapter Five

"We might as well close early, RaeAnn," Jaclyn told her office nurse. "We won't have more appointments or drop-ins this late. Besides I'm dead after being on call last night. Two heart attacks, a broken arm, a broken leg, suspected meningitis and an accident with a chain saw were enough." She grimaced. "Not that I'm complaining. At least people trust me in an emergency."

"They'll come around. Hang in there." RaeAnn patted her shoulder.

"That's what everyone says." Jaclyn pocketed her phone. "So far I feel like I'm hanging out to dry."

"Hey, where's your faith?" RaeAnn challenged. "God is working. You just have to give it time."

Time. Something Jaclyn was running short of with only two months left before she lost her funding. Unless Kent got her clinic ready in time.

"Well, if you're serious about quitting early, I'm going to enjoy a half hour of sun before I get to work on dinner." RaeAnn shut down the computers and grabbed her handbag.

"I'm going to have a nap. Then I have a supper meeting at a service club."

"Another one?" The nurse frowned. "You just got in with

that speech-making group. You're sure joining a lot of things. Don't you think you're taking on too much?"

"I'm trying to fit in so people will see I'm not the same dumb kid they once knew. And I haven't exactly joined the second service club yet. I'm still a guest," Jaclyn told her. "I'm hoping I can make a few friends there."

Except that no one hung around to talk to her after the meeting. Everyone seemed to have a place to be—except her. Jaclyn deliberately drove past the clinic site, as she had twice every day for the past two weeks. She was getting frustrated. How could she get patients if she didn't have a professional place to see them? That pokey room tucked into an unused corner of the hospital wasn't going to inspire confidence in new patients.

Jaclyn climbed out of her car and tried the door of the clinic but it was locked, and no one answered her knock. She'd hoped to work off some of her stress tonight by assisting Kent. Manual labor would go a long way toward making her feel like she hadn't lost all command of her world.

But Kent was not at the building. Again. Two whole weeks and as far as she could tell, nothing was happening with the clinic. Two weeks of no lights, no noises of construction, nothing. It was as if Kent had completely forgotten about her clinic.

Desperation edged in on her already strained nerves. When was he going to finish the place? Had he given up? And if he had, why didn't he just come right out and tell her?

"I'm trying to help," she said through gritted teeth. "What does it take to get some cooperation in this town, God?"

Fuming, Jaclyn climbed back in her car and headed for the McCloy ranch. If Kent had given up or changed his mind, she had to know now. Not that it was likely she could make alternate arrangements at this late date, but she couldn't just give up, either. She had to *do* something.

The scenic beauty on the drive to the ranch eased some of her frustration. The valleys burst with lushness. She reveled in the beauty of the hills, and was reminded of the days she and Jessica had saddled up and ridden over the hills of their own ranch, searching for a perfect patch to lie on and peer into the heavens, full of dreams and plans for the future.

Only Jessica never had the opportunity to fulfill her plans.

"I want you to live all the things I won't, Jaci," she'd said, lying in her bed. "Don't be angry at God. He knows what He's doing."

"Jess—" Her sister had stopped the words with a pale, thin finger against her lips.

"Do all the things we planned. Be a doctor, start the clinic. Live, Jaci. Do it for me. I love you." That night Jessica fell into a coma. She never awoke.

The only way Jaclyn could appease her pain was to take action. So Jaclyn worked, trying to earn the gift of life that had been taken away from her sister. She'd strived so hard to make her parents proud of her, but the pain of Jessica's loss was too great and they'd all fallen away from each other. Neither parent approved of her decision to return to Hope.

In the recesses of her mind, Jaclyn had never achieved Jessica's peace about God's failure to heal. That angst was bearable only when buried under a cloak of activity. She had to get Kent to complete the clinic.

In the McCloy ranch yard, heavily scented pink blossoms on fruit trees mingled with the blush of spring flowers newly opened, their whimsical fragrance filling the air. Kent's truck was parked in the side yard so he had to be around, though no one answered her knock.

Jaclyn headed around the side, toward the paddock, and saw him saddling a big bay stallion that danced with anticipation. Kent seemed totally engrossed in his task and never even looked up as she approached.

"How are you, Kent?"

"Hey." He blinked at her, smiled then continued cinching the saddle. "What are you doing out here?"

"I came to talk to you." When he didn't respond, she added, "About the clinic."

"You should have phoned. I would have told you I can't talk right now. I'm on the way to check on some cattle." His answers were short and brisk. He didn't look at her.

"But—"

"I'm busy right now." His tone made it clear he wasn't about to relinquish his plans.

"I'll go with you to check the cattle." The words slipped out without thought, but Jaclyn knew it was the right decision. "Maybe we can talk on the way." She looked toward the horses in the paddock. "Is there a certain one you'd prefer me to ride?"

"Jaclyn." Kent studied her for several moments. After a moment he sighed. "How long is it since you've ridden?"

"High school." She held steady under his stare, breathing deeply only when he turned away to whistle. A pretty chestnut mare trotted over.

"This is Tangay. She was Lisa's." Kent frowned. "Think you can handle her?"

"I'm sure she'll be fine." Confident words when she wasn't confident at all. Jaclyn hoped Kent couldn't tell.

"Not that I'm complaining, but are you going to ride in those clothes?" he asked in a careful tone.

She glanced down. "I have gym clothes in my car. I'll change and be back in a second."

"Use the house. I'll saddle her up." He waited until she'd walked about fifty feet before he asked, "Are you sure you want to come? It's not an easy ride."

"Kent." She tsk-tsked. "You should know nothing worthwhile ever is easy. You should certainly know that 'hard' doesn't stop me." She grinned at him then walked to her car.

In record time she'd changed into jogging pants, a cotton shirt and sneakers. Not exactly ideal riding wear, but it would do for now. When she returned to the corral, Kent was waiting, obviously eager to leave. He handed her the reins and offered her a boost up into the saddle.

"Hello, Tangay. Be gentle with me, will you? It's a long time since I went for a ride."

"You don't have a hat." Kent frowned.

"I doubt I'll get sun stroke this late in the afternoon."

"Are you sure—"

"Unless you want to get off that horse and talk to me here and now about the clinic, I'm going on this ride." She gave him the fiercest look she could manage.

"Okay, okay. Let's go." He led the way but glanced back to say, "But don't blame me if you're stiff and sore tomorrow."

"Like riding a bike," she said airily. "Nothing to it."

The dirt path soon disappeared. Kent motioned her to ride beside him.

Jaclyn reveled in the glorious green of the hillside. "Look at that valley. The sun's lit a kind of aura around it."

"Uh-huh." Apparently he was too used to it to get overly excited.

"Where are we going?"

"Sore already?" he teased, ignoring her dark look. "We're going over to Shadow Ridge. We used to go there for campfires with the youth group."

"I remember." Shadow Ridge was where she'd first asked the other kids to pray for Jessica.

"Some of my cattle trespassed onto my neighbor's property. Again. I need to see why." He made it sound as if it was a repeated chore he did not enjoy.

"How do you manage the cattle, all this land and your practice?" Jaclyn was beginning to understand Kent's reluctance to take on the clinic renovation. He had to be exhausted juggling so many demands on his time.

"I have help with the ranch," he told her. "Two men usually, but one is off sick and the other's on holiday. So today it's just me and the dumb cattle. Normally I don't have much interaction with them."

"Why is that?" Jaclyn caught an undertone in his voice. "You always loved animals."

"Most animals," he corrected. His mouth slanted down in a grim line. "I've never liked longhorns."

"Why?" The funny tone told Jaclyn there was a lot he wasn't saying.

"Since we moved to this ranch, I've been stabbed, kicked and mauled by longhorns."

"Surely that's not unusual. You must have had animals bite you. I've had kids do that. Part of the job." Jaclyn studied him. "Isn't it?"

"Maybe. It's a little different when you're staring down a two-thousand-pound animal with horns who just wants you out of the way." His voice grew tight. "I grit my teeth and treat them when I have to but that doesn't mean I like them."

"Then why keep longhorns on your ranch?" There was something Kent wasn't saying so Jaclyn pressed, even though she knew she shouldn't.

"Because they were Dad's." The words burst out of him in an annoyed rush. "He loved them, said they were a breed to honor. Dad spent hours choosing, trading one animal so he could get another." Kent adjusted his reins, avoiding her eyes. "I can't just get rid of his handpicked herd. It would be like selling the ranch."

Jaclyn didn't remember his father being so obsessed about cattle but then she hadn't known him that well. She rode in silence, struggling to recall Kent's parents. She remembered something else instead.

"Weren't you the guy whose yearbook blurb said he was going to build a petting zoo, or a sanctuary for wild animals? Something like that. What happened to that plan?"

"It's on hold." Kent stopped at a tiny stream and dismounted. He offered a hand to help her down. "Let them have a drink," he said. "Then we'll head up the hill."

Once she was off the horse, Jaclyn sank onto a big, flat sun-warmed rock. Kent would tell her the rest of the story when he was ready. She hoped.

He led the horses to the water. As they drank he ran a hand down his stallion's flanks, his touch gentle on the glossy black coat. Clearly he loved his horse, though he only patted Tangay once before moving away.

"Why didn't you sell Tangay?" she asked in the gloaming of the riverside.

"She's got medical issues. I couldn't charge anyone knowing that and there aren't many ranchers who want a problem horse."

"Is it okay for me to ride her?" Jaclyn worried.

"Oh, yeah. Tangay doesn't get enough exercise. But she's not up to anything more demanding than an occasional ride." Kent dragged off his black Stetson and raked a hand through the riot of curls that shone ebony. He sprawled on a nearby rock, a piece of grass in his mouth. Kent McCloy was a very handsome man.

"Thank you for bringing me here." Jaclyn inhaled the peace and beauty surrounding her. "I needed a break to readjust my thinking. You may have guessed I have control issues."

Kent raised one eyebrow, smiled, but said nothing.

"I need to have things arranged just so."

"I noticed." He winked at her.

"Well, I'm working on remembering God's in control." His wink had her flustered.

They sat in silence until Kent held out his hand to help her stand.

"Time to go," he said, his smile slightly crooked.

His touch against her skin sent a heat wave up her arm that had nothing to do with the waning sun. Jaclyn scrambled back on her horse, pretending nonchalance as they rode up the hill.

"There they are." He halted on the rise and pointed a finger at several cattle perfectly content to graze on someone else's land. "How— Oh, I see. The fence is damaged. I'll have to drive out with the truck tomorrow morning and fix it."

"I can help now if you want." Jaclyn saw his smile peek out before he composed his expression into a bland mask.

"Thanks, but I didn't bring my equipment." He shrugged. "This was just a trip to reconnoiter. Oh, look." He pointed to a sleek, dark form racing across the open. Then it slipped into the shadows of a clump of trees. His voice dropped to a whisper. "I think it's the same one."

"The same one what?" Jaclyn peered, but the gloomy shadows hid the animal.

"A wolf. I came out here about a month ago." Seeing the wolf, Kent's demeanor underwent a complete transformation. "A young wolf cub had injured himself and was trapped in some cactus brambles. Took me a while but I got him free, gave him some water and cleaned up his cut."

"He let you?"

"I think he realized he had nothing to fear from me. Whenever I come to this area, I usually see him. I always leave something for him so now I guess he's come to expect a treat." He dug in his saddle bag and pulled out a plastic zipper bag. "This won't take long."

Jaclyn watched him remove a large steak. Kent laid it on

a boulder, tucked the bag back into his pocket and got back on his horse.

"He'll wait till we're away from here then he'll come over to check. Do you want to watch?"

"Yes." Jaclyn followed Kent for a minute, then they dismounted and sat on the ground, holding the horses' reins.

"I've come across lots of different injured animals since we moved here when I was a kid," he told her, his voice low and even. "I try to help them if I can. Some of them remember." His hand stilled hers as she reached to touch her hair. "Don't make any sudden moves."

"What kind of a wolf is it?" she breathed.

"Mexican wolf. Not too many of them left. Come on, fella. Come and taste your dinner." Kent kept up a low monotone until the animal emerged from the woods and loped toward them. "Okay?" he asked.

"Stunned, but yes. I'm fine." She tightened her grip on the reins as Tangay shifted. "It's okay, girl. I think this is a friend."

"It is," Kent assured her. "He'll inspect the area first. He doesn't know your scent so he may be a bit shy. But the scent of that meat will bug him and eventually he'll take it. Just don't move."

"Not going anywhere," Jaclyn whispered and threaded her fingers through his without even thinking about it. When she realized what she'd done, she hesitated. But she could hardly jerk her hand away now. "Here he comes. How his coat shines."

The wolf halted about fifty feet in front of them, lifted his head and sniffed the air.

"Talk calmly. Don't raise your voice or you'll frighten him. He's not a people person."

She leaned close to Kent's ear and whispered, "I'm not sure I'm a wolf person, but I'll try to behave properly."

Kent's eyes met hers in a connection that sent frissons of shock waves straight to her heart. He didn't let go of her hand until Tangay's whinny broke the spell that held them.

"Give me those." He slid the reins from her nerveless fingers and with a whisper calmed the horse.

The wolf studied them from his safe vantage point. Kent studied him just as hard. Riveted by the expression on the vet's handsome face, Jaclyn couldn't look away. This was a Kent she'd never seen.

"Look, our boy is coming a little closer." Kent's lips grazed her ear. "Stay as still as you can."

Breath suspended, Jaclyn watched the wolf pace off the area, constantly sniffing, occasionally lifting his head to check out some movement. Finally he stopped about twenty feet away from Kent's left side.

"Hello, big fella. You're looking good. You been riding herd on my cattle?" The wolf tossed his head. Kent grinned. "Well, thank you. I appreciate that. I left you a little snack. I know hunting's not as good as it once was. A guy has to work hard to get a decent meal, doesn't he?"

Jaclyn didn't move, entranced by Kent. His entire demeanor altered as he interacted with the animal. The irritation that had permeated his behavior when he'd talked about the longhorns was completely gone. Now his voice was full of tenderness. Totally relaxed and in the moment with this magnificent wild animal, Kent's face radiated bliss.

"You enjoy your dinner, fella. And take care of yourself. We'll meet again."

The wolf waited a moment, as if to signal his agreement then loped toward the steak. After several sniffs he grabbed the meat in his powerful jaws and raced across the valley, heading into the trees. He turned once to look back, as if to say thanks, then disappeared. When she could see him no more, Jaclyn finally let out her pent-up breath.

"That was amazing!"

"Yeah." Kent grinned at her. "They're incredible animals. Clever, resourceful and extremely intelligent."

"He certainly responded to you. I've never seen anything like that before." She looked at him carefully. "You should get to work on your animal shelter—you do still want to build a sanctuary, don't you?"

"Yes." He sat up. "I often get to treat injured wild animals but they usually end up going to a zoo or something. If there was an area where they could be free instead of confined to cages or stalls…" His voice drifted away.

"Forget those longhorns, Kent. Your calling lies elsewhere. I think your father, if he were here, would agree."

"My father was all about ranching." Ice cracked his voice.

"But—"

Kent cut her off. "We should head back before it gets dark." He helped her rise and handed Tangay's reins to her. "Ready?"

The vibrancy that had transformed his face and sparkled in his sapphire eyes dissipated. The impassioned wild-animal caregiver had changed into a cattleman doing his duty.

Oh, Kent.

But all Jaclyn said was, "Ready." She mounted up.

He led her back on a different route, this time more open with sweeping vistas on all sides. The silence between them stretched until they arrived at the rear entrance to his ranch.

"You know, I understand why you came back to the ranch." She felt oddly diminished and yet expanded by the beauty of his land. "I feel very close to God out here."

"Do you?"

"It's almost like I can reach out and touch Him."

Kent didn't respond.

As she followed him into the barn, she noticed blackened sticks poking from the earth. "How did the fire start?" she asked quietly.

"Lightning. It was a very dry year and everything went up like tinder." His voice hardened, his words emerging short, clipped. Gone was the gentle whisper. Cold, hard anger burned in his eyes as he removed their saddles. "Once lit, the wildfire became massive." His fingertips whitened as he gripped the curry brush and swept it down his horse's sides.

She wanted him to talk about it, to let out the festering hurt. That's what the counselor had told her parents when Jessica died, though they'd never done it, at least not in Jaclyn's presence. Maybe that's why they were so far apart now.

"And Lisa got caught in it." Jaclyn began brushing Tangay.

"Not exactly caught." He stopped brushing and inhaled. When he spoke again, his words emerged in tight, controlled snaps. "I lit a backfire to stop the wildfire. It was so dry. We didn't have enough water. I was desperate. The barns, the sheds, maybe even the house were in its path."

"So you had to cut off its fuel." Jaclyn waited while he put the horses in the paddock to nibble on the fresh grass. "Do you have any iced tea? I'm terribly thirsty." She didn't want to leave him with the sad memory of Lisa's death. He needed to talk; she needed to listen. Maybe that was the only way she could help him. "What I don't understand is why Lisa would go out in it."

"Nor do I." He waited till she was seated at the kitchen table before sitting opposite her. Condensation ran down their glasses and puddled on the table. He studied the surface, avoiding Jaclyn's eyes. "I doubt I ever will."

"Maybe she didn't understand what you were going to do?" Jaclyn suggested.

"She understood. I told her. And yet she walked right into it." He sucked in a breath. "I'd already lit the fire when I saw her. I tried to reach her, but it caught fast and I couldn't control it." His gravelly voice became hoarse. "I couldn't get to her. The flames were too much."

"You saw her?" Horror shuddered through her at his nod. She could only imagine carrying that image around every day and the blame that would magnify over time. Jaclyn took his hand, cradling his icy fingers, speaking fast, urgently. "You listen to me. It was not your fault, Kent. Do you hear me? It was not your fault."

"Whose then?" The bleakness in his voice matched the utter despair in his dark eyes. "God's? Hers?" He gazed at their clasped fingers then slowly drew his hand away. "I made her stay here. Lisa never wanted to come back to the ranch. But after Mom and Dad died, I had to come here, to straighten things out and try to make a go of it. I owed them that."

"You were their son, Kent. Of course you handled their estate." His tortured voice touched the deepest part of Jaclyn's heart. She'd suffered with Jessica's death, but at least she'd never felt she caused it.

"I didn't have to stay here." His head lifted and he stared at her.

"What do you mean?" Jaclyn didn't understand the blazing anger on his face.

"I could have sold everything and left. But I broke my promise to Lisa that we'd go back to Texas. I kept her in a place where she was desperately unhappy. And do you know why, Jaclyn?" Harsh laughter cracked the silence as he waited for her answer. "Of course you don't. Nobody does."

"Kent, this is upsetting you and I never meant to do that." She wished she hadn't pushed him to talk just to satisfy her need to know what happened.

"Can't take the truth, huh?" His smile didn't reach his eyes.

"I blamed myself for Jessica's death wondering if I would have done this or that, if it would have made a difference. But it wouldn't have—it couldn't have. So you go on."

"Is that what you're doing?" Bitterness flashed in those vivid blue eyes. "Are you going on with your life, Jaclyn? Is joining every group you can the way you're getting on with your life? Or are you postponing your life so you can make amends?"

She bit her lip at the accusation. "Stop it."

After a moment, Kent touched her hand, his face ashen. "I'm really sorry. I'm lashing out at you and you don't deserve it." He shook his head. "Let's just leave it alone, okay?"

"Okay." *For now,* she thought. But sooner or later she'd discover why he felt duty bound to keep his father's cattle, and why he'd stayed here when he could have left. This man was in deep pain and she ached to help him. If only she could figure out how. "So, the reason I came out tonight was to talk about the clinic. Is there anything I can do to help get it moving again?"

"No." He sighed. "I was waiting on some material. I heard this afternoon that it's in so I'll be back there tomorrow." His voice was devoid of all emotion.

"Thank you, Kent. I appreciate all you've done." She rose. "I need to get home. I've got a meeting. Thanks for the ride."

"Sure." He walked her to her car, silent and darkly brooding.

"Call me if you need help. With anything." He didn't respond. All Jaclyn could do was drive away. She glanced and saw him standing there, alone.

Something's wrong, God. It's like he's drowning. Please help him, she prayed as she drove down the hill and back into town. *Please help me to help him. And most of all please help the clinic. I've got to get it running.*

The prayer made her feel a bit selfish. How could she push her own agenda when Kent seemed so broken?

She recalled the touch of his hands on hers, the protective way he'd helped her on and off Tangay. Most of all she remembered the way he'd stood there, alone, watching her leave. She'd wanted to turn around, go back and assure him he wasn't alone.

But she couldn't. Jaclyn couldn't afford to get sidetracked by Kent McCloy. Besides, she knew what happened to love. It died, just the way Brianna and Zac's had, and the way her parents' had, so that now it seemed as if they barely tolerated each other. Romantic love didn't last and Jaclyn had no intention of going down that path. Still, her heart longed to find a way to help Kent.

Nothing wrong with that. As long as she didn't let it become more than friendship.

Chapter Six

Kent drove through Hope the next morning with a sinking feeling in his stomach that had begun at 7:15 a.m. with Heddy's phone call.

"Can you be at the library at ten-thirty, Kent? We need to talk."

During his first months as mayor, he'd learned that ignoring Heddy's demands was done at his own peril. So now, as he pulled into the library parking lot, he hoped she'd get it over with quickly, whatever it was. He had plans to spend some time on the clinic today. Jaclyn was right—he had been putting it off, mostly because finding the trades he needed seemed impossible. But he wasn't giving up. Not yet.

Kent had barely crossed the threshold of the library when he spotted Jaclyn. He jerked to a halt at the sight of her sitting on the floor, surrounded by preschoolers, their faces rapt as they listened to her.

"Quite a sight, isn't it?" Heddy directed him into a room where he could still see Jaclyn through the floor-to-ceiling windows. "She's a natural storyteller."

"Is that what you wanted to talk to me about?" Kent tried to keep his gaze from straying to the pretty blonde and her big, wide smile, but Jaclyn was a magnet that constantly drew his attention. She looked perfectly at home on the floor, as if she was having as much fun as the kids were.

"Certainly speaks to her character."

"It does?" Kent blinked. Heddy was now the doctor's champion? His instincts went on alert. "Why?"

"Jaclyn heard our story-time team couldn't show and volunteered to help." Heddy's face glowed as he hadn't seen it in ages. "She's an amazing woman."

"Also a very good doctor. So why don't you use her services, or tell your daughter to?" he challenged.

"I intend to do both." Heddy smiled at his surprise. "Why not? My grandchildren need a good physician nearby."

Kent was dumbfounded.

"Oh, don't look at me like that," Heddy scolded. "Aren't you the one who's been telling everyone in this town to look at things in a new way?"

"I have." He never imagined Heddy had taken his comments seriously.

"Well, I have examined my attitude and decided to change it." She sighed. "I admit it's taken me a long time to get past what happened all those years ago. You have to understand, Jaclyn wrecked the doors which my grandfather donated to the church." Heddy's face lost some of its glow. "Those doors commemorated the death of his wife—my grandmother— and I loved her dearly."

"You don't have to explain to me, Heddy." Kent was surprised by a rush of compassion for the woman who had so often made his life a misery.

"I do." She dabbed her eyes and cleared her throat. "I watched my grandfather sacrifice to buy those doors—he endured hardship to commemorate his wife's life. Every time I went into that church, I looked at those doors and relived so many happy memories of my grandmother."

"I see."

"Those doors cost a mint to refinish and even when they were done, they were never the same." Heddy sniffed.

"I'm sorry, Heddy. And I know Jaclyn is."

"Yes, she apologized to me back then but I never believed she was genuinely sorry. But after hearing Jaclyn talk about losing her sister—I could see how her hurt still hasn't left her." Heddy's gaze pinned him. "Kent, she doesn't want the clinic because she's trying to make a name for herself. She's trying to make amends for living."

He frowned, hoping Heddy wouldn't spread that insight around town.

"When she talked about the bond she had with her twin, it made me realize I'd never accepted that she was mourning way back then." Heddy shrugged. "So when Jaclyn called yesterday to offer to have the doors refinished, I refused."

Pride surged up in Kent that Jaclyn had reached out to Heddy. He turned to look at Jaclyn.

"Are you listening?" Heddy demanded when Kent didn't respond right away.

"Why did you refuse?" he asked patiently.

"Doors are just things and Grandfather never put things above people." Heddy beamed. "I've forgiven Jaclyn."

"That's very generous of you." Kent could hardly contain his amazement. In the years since he'd been in Hope he'd never known Heddy to openly forgive anyone until she'd exacted whatever retribution she felt entitled to. Yet Jaclyn had softened her heart in a matter of a few weeks.

"It's very generous of Jaclyn to give us this clinic," Heddy said.

Laughter penetrated the glass windows. When Kent looked, he saw the kids doubled over with the giggles. Jaclyn was making faces.

"Whatever she's reading them seems to be a hit," he said.

"Oh, she's not reading anything." Heddy's pale eyes danced

with excitement. "Not yet. She's giving them a talk about health."

"Health?"

"Yes. She has this fuzzy worm, Ernesto. And she's been using him—well, just look. You can see for yourself." Heddy tilted her head sideways, indicating the circle of children now avidly involved in what was happening.

Kent looked at the doctor clad in her white coat, a green wiggling puppet covering one hand. Just then Jaclyn glanced up, saw him and winked. Every single mom nearby turned to look at him. Even Heddy grinned.

Kent's face burned.

"She has an amazing knack with kids." Heddy chuckled when one little boy cuddled onto Jaclyn's lap. She wrapped her free arm around the child and continued speaking, unfazed. "I never imagined she'd know how to reach them," Heddy said. "To look at her, you'd think she was all about fashion."

Another snap judgment, just like his. Kent winced. It wasn't just Heddy who'd been unfair. But as he stood watching her, he wondered if Jaclyn had agreed to fill in this morning in a deliberate attempt to win over moms and kids for her clinic.

He immediately chastised himself for the thought. What did it matter? The doctor had found a way to fit in here. He found himself feeling proud of her again.

Though he had no business feeling anything for Jaclyn LaForge.

"So what did you want to talk to me about, Heddy?" Kent was desperate to leave so he could get his attention off the doctor.

"The Pruitt boy." Heddy pursed her lips. "His mom told me this morning that Jaclyn is insisting Joey sees a specialist."

"That's a good thing." He saw her frown. "Isn't it?"

"No. That family was decimated when the boy was injured. You've seen how many times they've hoped for some new treatment and then had their hopes dashed." Her eyes misted. "Those poor people have been on a roller coaster. Each time they see another specialist it happens again, but the result is the same. Joey's condition is untreatable."

Kent had heard that, too.

"The family has come to grips with Joey's problems and Joey's adapted. Another examination, another test—it won't help. It will only get their hopes up only to have them crushed again."

"You told Jaclyn?" Heddy nodded. "What did she say?"

"She won't listen to me."

"Jaclyn's the doctor. I'm only a vet. I'd no more ask Jaclyn to listen to my advice about her patients than I would take hers about mine."

"Be that as it may, you must try to dissuade her about this," Heddy insisted. Her fingers closed around his wrist.

He didn't get this. "You just said you trusted Jaclyn. I thought you'd be glad she's taking an interest in the boy's treatment." He drew his arm away from her tight fingers.

Heddy's eyes brimmed with sadness. "I know you don't believe it, but I want this town to heal and I'm trying to help."

"How?" He didn't understand the source of Heddy's fierce glower.

"Think and you'll realize the damage this could do, to Dr. LaForge, to Joey and to his family. The doctors have all said the same thing. Joey's spine was damaged too badly in the car accident. He'll never walk properly."

"I'm sure Dr. LaForge has that information in Joey's records," he said.

"Then why does she want Joey to see someone else?" An indulgent smile creased her mouth. "I want her clinic to succeed. But if she keeps pushing the Pruitts, she'll only get their hopes up and when they're disappointed again, the whole town will turn on Jaclyn." There were tears at the corners of Heddy's eyes. "Hope will suffer again, Kent. Jaclyn has good intentions but please, ask her to stop."

He studied her, surprised by Heddy's about-face to Jaclyn's side.

"It may be a moot point," he told her.

"What do you mean?"

"Jaclyn must open her clinic by May and right now it looks like that won't happen because I can't get an electrician to certify the building." He waited for the usual caustic comment, but Heddy surprised him.

"Well, of course her clinic will open. It can't be that hard to get an electrician. My son is one. A very good one." She preened. "He even has his own company over in Whiteville."

"I know. But your son isn't here. Hope's only two electricians are at the mine and can't be released from a noncompete contract." He held up a hand when she would have interrupted. "I've tried asking. The mine company made an exception for the plumber but they won't allow this. If I can't get that building rewired, I can't let Jaclyn move in. And if she doesn't move in, her clinic won't happen. She may even be forced to move away."

Heddy was finally silenced.

"So you probably have nothing to worry about." Kent shrugged, pretending it didn't matter to him, when in reality he absolutely did not want Jaclyn to leave. She made a difference in his life and he had begun to like that.

Heddy was silent for a long time. Her birdlike gaze moved from him to Jaclyn, to the mothers sipping their coffee, and back to him. Finally she spoke.

"If I can get whatever electrical work is needed in that clinic done, will you ask Jaclyn to stop pushing the Pruitts to see another specialist?"

When he didn't answer, she poked his chest.

"Is it a deal, Kent?"

He made up his mind in an instant.

"If you promise to get the wiring done, I'll talk to Jaclyn. But it's very unlikely she will discuss a patient with me. I'm not a medical doctor, Heddy. I don't keep up with the latest treatments. But I'm sure Jaclyn does. She may know of something that can help the boy." He gulped, stunned by his own temerity. "I'll try to find out why she's so determined to get Joey to another specialist, but if she insists on going ahead, that's her business."

She patted his shoulder. "Thank you, Kent. I know Jaclyn feels a close connection with you, probably because you're the only one of us that's been a real friend to her. That's why I thought this admonishment would sound better coming from you than me."

"Heddy!" he sputtered in outrage. "I'm not going to admonish—"

"I must go. It's snack time."

Heddy scurried away so fast Kent felt like he'd been had. At least he got an electrician out of the deal. He only hoped it wouldn't backfire.

"Hi. Do you come to story time often?" Jaclyn stood in front of him, amused.

"Only when Heddy summons me." Jaclyn was radiant. Her eyes sparkled with happiness. "Looked like you were having fun."

"I was. I love kids." She tilted her head to one side. "And you?"

"Me? Yeah, I like kids. Listen, Jaclyn, have you got time for a coffee?" Better to get this over with. But he wasn't going to challenge whatever decision she made.

"I have no patients this morning, but I may have gained one or two today." She tossed him a wink. Her teasing smile died away when he didn't respond. She grabbed her bag and followed him out of the library.

As Kent walked with her to the nearest café, it dawned on him that he knew little about Jaclyn personally beyond her desire to get the clinic operational. She always coaxed him to talk about himself. In the café, Jaclyn held her cup and stared him down.

"What's going on, Kent? What's this about?"

"Heddy. And the Pruitts." He launched in, relaying Heddy's worries bluntly, embarrassed he'd agreed to be part of this. "So I said I'd mention it to you."

"Okay. Now you have." She rose and reached for her purse.

"Jaclyn, I'm not trying to tell you how to practice medicine." Kent touched her arm.

"Good," she snapped. "Because you're not qualified."

Uh-oh, she was steaming. Well, who wouldn't be? He'd questioned her professional judgment. And yet he also wanted to save her grief, if he could.

"Please sit down, Jaclyn. Finish your coffee and talk to me about this."

She sat. But the firm jut of her chin told Kent his soft tones weren't working.

"I do not discuss my patients," she said. "You should know that."

"I do know. And I respect it. But I've known the Pruitts and Joey for years. I've seen what they go through each time their hopes are built up and what happens when they're dashed. I've watched the people of this town rally round them." Kent struggled to voice his thoughts inoffensively. "We might bicker and argue among ourselves in Hope, but underneath we still feel responsible and look out for each other."

Her eyes glittered like polished granite. "Why the sudden concern about me trying to do my job? Last night you were all gung ho about encouraging me. You told me to have faith. Now you're questioning my ability to do my job."

"No!" He backtracked. "I just wanted to be sure that you knew—"

Hurt filled Jaclyn's eyes. A nerve flickered in her neck as she steeled herself and in that moment Kent wished he'd never started this because now there was no way to make it right. He'd overstepped the bounds and he knew it.

"It's none of my business. I'm very sorry, Jaclyn," he said simply.

She studied him for so long he wanted to squirm under that look.

"Thank you—for that, at least." Then she rose and walked out.

Kent spent a long time with his coffee. It took a while to examine his heart and realize that he'd just hurt Jaclyn to spare himself. He'd grabbed at Heddy's offer to get an electrician because he wanted to get the clinic finished. He wanted to get Jaclyn moved in so he wouldn't have to go through another visit like she'd made last night, wouldn't ever again have to risk her seeing his weaknesses. He wanted her office finished so he could feel he'd done something for the town. Mostly he wanted to get back to the hermit's life he'd carved out before Dr. Jaclyn LaForge crashed his world.

But his crime, Kent admitted to himself, was worse than that. Far worse. He'd spouted off to a whole lot of people, including Heddy and Jaclyn herself, that he trusted her judgment, that he was confident she was the doctor for Hope. Pretty words. But his actions made a total lie of what he'd said. And though she'd said not a word to condemn him, Jaclyn knew it.

Kent paid for the two untouched coffees and walked out of the café. Okay, he'd messed up badly. Guilt rose as he realized that if there was any chance for Joey, he might have just killed it. No wonder God had washed His hands of Kent McCloy.

His mouth grim, Kent headed for the clinic and got to work. It was time to put his money where his mouth was, though even if he got the clinic finished in time, it wouldn't likely restore Jaclyn's opinion of him.

Jaclyn sat behind her desk and studied the file of Joey Pruitt. The sting of Kent's questioning haunted her. She'd been furious at first and had itched to tell him to mind his own business. Fortunately, Jaclyn's temper had cooled in the past few hours. Kent's lack of belief still stung, but it also had her second-guessing her decision to pursue help for Joey Pruitt.

Kent wasn't a physician. Yet his and Heddy's concern over what the Pruitt family might have to go through was obviously genuine. She'd seen the rush of hope flicker in the parents' eyes when she'd first mentioned the specialist. She'd also seen the way they ruthlessly tamped it down to ask all the hard questions and then asked her not to tell Joey anything until they'd made a decision.

Jaclyn knew the painful rehabilitation Joey would have to go through if the surgery worked. But what if it didn't? What if it left him worse off than before? What if the whole town turned against her because of that?

My job is to find healing. I can't worry what people will think of me.

There were no guarantees in medicine.

Jaclyn phoned the specialist to talk over the case before she requested they schedule Joey for an appointment. If his parents decided to cancel, that was their decision.

Was there anything else she could do? Yes, pray.

I don't know what the outcome will be, God. I only know that You love children and You want them to be well.

RaeAnn ducked her head in to say it was five and she was leaving.

"What are you doing tonight?" her nurse asked.

"I'm going to finish this paperwork then reorganize my file cabinet." Jaclyn pointed to the stack of files on the floor. "And I have to phone that list of people for the service club."

"Always busy," RaeAnn grumbled, then said good-night.

Jaclyn quickly completed her to-do list, but she couldn't stop thinking about Kent. Last night she'd seen a different side of the man. The way he'd changed at the appearance of the wolf stunned her. So had his angst about the getting rid of the longhorns. It was laudable that Kent wanted to honor his parent, but something else underlay his anguish.

She left the office and drove past the clinic, shocked that the lights were on and Kent's truck was parked outside. Should she offer her help again? No. He'd said he'd do it, now leave him alone.

Only, he always seemed to be alone.

Jaclyn drove home, made herself a sandwich and ate it while she watched the news. She wondered if Kent was eating, if he'd eaten all day. She finally changed into jeans, wrapped a sandwich, grabbed two bottles of juice and made a quick phone call. Then she walked downtown. The fragrance of flowering shrubs filled the air and fireflies flitted past as she waved at passersby, delighted that she could identify most of them.

She stopped outside the clinic's new glass door, brimming with second thoughts. Why was she doing this? Kent had hurt her deeply. He'd questioned her judgment. He'd claimed to trust her, to want her to succeed, but then put up barriers. Bringing him a sandwich would make her seem desperate.

He cares about the people in this town.

He's a good man.

He's hurting inside. He's lost his wife, his parents—he has no one.

"All right," she mumbled, exasperated by the amount of inner conflict one man could cause.

"Talking to yourself?" Kent stood holding the door open with one booted toe, his arms filled with junk.

"You're working here again." It was an inane remark and Jaclyn blushed at the stupidity of it.

"Free evening," he said before he tossed the broken boards into a Dumpster that sat in a parking spot. "I thought I'd get a couple of hours in."

"Oh." She trailed behind him into the room, surprised by how much lighter it felt without the dark paneling.

"On your way home with dinner?" he asked. He inclined his head toward the bag she held.

"No, I've already eaten. I thought perhaps you hadn't." She held out the bag then faltered. "Or maybe you have."

"I haven't," he said and took the bag from her. "In fact, I'm starving."

"Good." She handed him one of the juice bottles and watched as he unwrapped the sandwich.

"Thank you." He held up the sandwich, staring at it. "Jaclyn, I need to apologize to you. I never should have questioned your judgment about Joey. My only excuse is that Heddy promised me an electrician if I did and I got carried away by the prospect of actually getting this place rewired and certified. I'm sorry."

"Where's Heddy going to find an electrician?" She glanced around at the broken walls, dangling fixtures and utter chaos.

Kent kept looking at her, his blue eyes dark, worried. "You haven't said you've forgiven me," he reminded.

"You expect a lot." Jaclyn glared at him, irritation bubbling up anew. "I can take criticism, Kent. I understand that the locals are worried I'll take off at the first hint of a better job. I can understand their distrust of my motives. I even understand that they don't want Joey or his parents to get their hopes dashed again." The hurt was still there, raw, throbbing. "What I can't take is a friend questioning my medical judgment. You crossed the line, Kent."

"I know I did. And I'm sorry." He sat there, looking at her.

"Why did you do it? And don't say for an electrician."

"It was, partly. Progress here has been sporadic, and that's being generous." He sighed. "Mostly it was concern for you. I've seen what this town can do to protect their own. I don't want you to be the target of their anger."

"It wouldn't matter if I was," she said quietly. "I'd still do what's right for my patient. I took an oath and I promised God. That's why I'm in Hope. To help."

A long silence yawned between them. Kent's blue eyes wouldn't release hers. He seemed to see past her bravado to the secret fears beneath. Finally he nodded.

"I know," he said. "I apologize." Then he took a bite of the sandwich.

"Just like that?" She didn't believe him. "Why?"

"Because you're right." He munched thoughtfully for a minute then shrugged. "Bottom line, if there's even the remotest chance Joey can be helped, it's worth taking." He lifted his head when the door pushed open and Zac stepped inside. "Hey, Professor."

Zac winked at her. Jaclyn grinned, glad she'd phoned him.

"What are you doing here?" Kent asked.

"I'm here to help this damsel in distress." Zac made a motion as if he were doffing a hat. "At your service, Doc."

"Thank you for coming." She loved Kent's confusion. For once the town's do-gooder was flummoxed. "Where should we start?"

"Wait a minute." Kent rose. "What's going on?"

"We're going to give you a little push getting this place operational," Zac said. "Right, Doc?"

"Right. I—" She stopped as the door opened. A man stepped inside. "Can I help you?"

"You're the new doctor, right?" He held out his hand. "Paul Cormer. I was told you need some electrical work done here."

"Excellent!" Zac nudged Kent. "C'mon, cowboy, show him. We've got a clinic to fix."

Jaclyn nearly laughed out loud at Kent's stunned expression. When Kent and Paul disappeared to look at the panel box, she and Zac began hauling out the accumulated refuse.

"How'd we get this electrician?" Kent demanded when he returned as Zac took a bag outside. "The mine bosses were adamant none of their guys could work here. Did you change their minds?"

"Me? What do I know about electricians?" Jaclyn blinked. "It had to be Heddy."

"Changing the mine bosses' minds?" He shook his head. "Even Heddy doesn't have that much pull." His shoulder grazed hers. He took the garbage bag from her hands and held it while she filled it, his fingers brushing against hers. "You think?"

"Who else is there?" Jaclyn struggled to control her breathing. Lately she couldn't seem to control any of her responses to him. Just a touch from him and her nerves came alive. She rushed outside with the bag, inhaling the fresh air in an attempt to regain her equanimity.

"You look funny. Are you okay?" Zac asked.

"Uh-huh." She was far from okay. Her heart hammered in her chest; her head felt woozy and funny little prickles ran up and down her arm where Kent had touched her.

"If you say so." Zac frowned.

Jaclyn took her time, waiting for him to return inside. Finally alone she sat down on the curb and practiced relaxation breathing. But it didn't help. Nothing did.

Because the truth was too hard to digest, and impossible to accept.

She was starting to care for Kent McCloy.

"Hey, Jaclyn? We could use your help here." Kent's voice broke through her reverie.

"Coming." She went inside, but while she helped, she made a mental list of all the things she could do to keep away from this building. Away from Kent.

And she knew she wouldn't do a single one of them.

Chapter Seven

"Jaclyn, this cake looks delicious," the minister's wife praised. "Everyone's going to enjoy it."

"Good. That's why I made it." Well, that and the need to keep busy. She waved an airy hand as if baking a layer cake was something she did every day instead of a major job requiring many hours, in spite of using a cake mix and store-bought icing.

"Would you be in charge of the desserts for the potluck today?"

In charge of *them*? Meaning serving them?

"Sure," Jaclyn assured the busy woman.

"Thanks. I'll find someone to help you load them later." She scurried away.

Load them?

Jaclyn tried to recall how the last potluck lunch had worked but came up blank. Oh, well. Couldn't be that hard. She stopped in the foyer to drop the quilt squares she'd cut for the quilting meeting tomorrow into the appropriate box. The task had taken five evenings and she was glad to be finished with the tiring work.

"Jaclyn!" Heddy's voice boomed across the crowded foyer. "I hope you have those notes on leprosy that you promised me. Our missions' group wants to learn all we can so we can better prepare our care package for the missionaries."

"I have your information here." She drew the sheaf of notes from her bag and handed them over, relieved at the lightness of her purse.

"You are coming to the meeting? We need everyone's help."

"I'll try to be there." Jaclyn had joined so many groups she now needed a calendar to keep the meetings straight. Unfortunately she didn't have it with her and she didn't want to embarrass herself by asking Heddy which day.

In fact, she'd prefer to avoid Heddy altogether.

Jaclyn knew she'd taken on too much but refused to cut back. Sooner or later Hope-ites would see her as an integral part of Hope.

Jaclyn looked forward to relaxing and enjoying the service, but as she walked into the sanctuary, Heddy followed.

"How's work on the clinic?" She slid into the pew beside Jaclyn.

"You'd have to ask Kent." *Because I'm deliberately avoiding him.*

"Dear Kent. He's such a boon to this town. His concern is for all of us and he goes out of his way to make Hope a better place. It's a pity he hasn't anyone special in his life. He's such a handsome man, too."

Please God, let someone invite Heddy to sit with them.

"Have you heard Kent's taken in six miniature horses?" Heddy leaned nearer as the organ swelled. "They were abandoned, if you can imagine such a thing. That boy has such a heart." Heddy patted her hand. "Say, you're not working today, are you? You're just the person to help."

"Help with what?" Jaclyn asked warily.

"Transport food to the potluck, of course. It's at Kent's ranch. Surely you knew that?" Heddy ignored Jaclyn's sudden silence and peered across the room. "Excuse me. I must speak with Millie. We'll expect your help later, shall we?" She hurried away.

At Kent's.

If only she'd planned something pressing after church, but this was the one day Jaclyn had kept totally free. When she saw the outside of the church, she was always assailed by memories of that awful night and the vandalism she'd wreaked. Inside, she waited for memories of tranquility to quiet her soul. Instead a panoramic slideshow of Kent at his ranch played through her brain while the choir sang their first selection.

Kent petting his horse. Kent playing with the dog. Kent speaking so tenderly to the wolf.

Kent touching her hand and leaving behind an earthquake of emotion.

Okay, so she was falling for him. But why? A high school crush was one thing, but she was all grown up now. What was it about him?

On the day of their horse ride, when he'd envisioned an animal sanctuary, he'd exposed a part of his spirit she'd never seen before. As she considered his abrupt shut down of that dream, she realized Kent had substituted Hope's dreams for his own.

Having seen that transformation, Jaclyn now realized how much Kent was giving up. She'd seen the guilt take over, guilt so strong that he willingly relinquished his dreams. This generous, giving man had nobody in his world to help him achieve his goals, no one to encourage him to explore the dreams he'd held for so long. He gave but who gave to him?

For days Jaclyn had been trying to skate around her response to Kent, to avoid him and anything that would trigger her overwhelming reactions to him, because those feelings made her yearn to help him. She so longed to see him whole and happy that it scared her to think she might be persuaded to put aside her own goals.

If she allowed herself to get involved with Kent McCloy, those feelings would develop and all her dreams for the clinic would dwindle. Then she'd never earn the approval she'd craved ever since Jessica's death—not from her parents and not from herself. And getting that approval was the only way she'd feel she was worthy of the life Jessica never got to live.

The service began. Jaclyn sang the choruses from memory. She closed her eyes for prayer but her mind would not quiet. A thousand questions raced around it until the minister's voice broke through.

"Spring is God's way of saying, 'Let's start again.' It's His promise that after the drought, after the hard times, there will be beauty and sweetness once more. Spring can also be a time to examine our personal growth. Where are we going? What are we striving for? It's time to ask ourselves if our plan for the future is all about us or centered on God's will for us. Are we willing to change our plan, to give up parts of it, to accept failure if God gives a new vision, a new plan?"

As she listened, Jaclyn scribbled notes. The thought that she might be off course, or worse, completely mistaken in her plans unsettled her. Was that why getting the clinic operational was so difficult? Now she was questioning her dreams.

At the completion of the service, Jaclyn reluctantly loaded the desserts for transport to Kent's ranch. And during the potluck picnic she studied him surreptitiously. But her feelings were no clearer as she helped clean up his sterile kitchen. How could she possibly help him—yet stay true to herself and her path?

"I can't think of a way to throw the kind of party my daughter wants," Carissa, a young mother, lamented to the women cleaning up Kent's kitchen.

"What kind of a party does she want?" one of the other ladies asked.

"Casey was so sick for the past two years, she wasn't able to celebrate," Carissa said. She smiled at Jaclyn. "Thanks to our fantastic pediatrician who finally straightened out her medical issues, Casey can celebrate this year."

"A little tweak, that's all," Jaclyn murmured.

"Some really big tweaks nobody else thought of. I'll always be grateful you came to Hope, Jaclyn." Carissa grinned. "Now Casey wants to make up for what she missed—she wants to do something big. I want that, too, but other than hauling her friends to a Las Cruces waterpark, I'm stuck."

Jaclyn looked out the window and watched as Kent and another man walked to the paddock with the miniature horses. The man carried a child and the three paused by the fence.

The idea sprang full-blown. Miniature horses, pets galore. And a man who needed taking out of himself. Perfect.

"Maybe Kent would host the party here." Jaclyn was barely aware she'd spoken aloud until the other women crowded around her to watch Kent carry the girl inside the corral and show her how to feed the horse a carrot.

"Jaclyn, that's a fantastic idea!" Carissa hugged her. "Kent's amazing with kids. Look at the way he's teaching Emma."

With gentle patience he allowed the child to experience the animal close up.

"You could plan lots of games to wear off some of the kids' energy," another mom offered.

"Remember when Lisa hosted her barbecues here?" another said.

"We let her do too much," Carissa said. "That probably didn't help her depression."

"I'd be depressed, too, if I had to work in this kitchen

for very long," a woman named Amanda grumbled. "It's so sterile."

They all studied the cold room.

"It is very efficient," Jaclyn said. "All it needs is some color to warm it up."

The ideas continued fast and furious. If her goal was to waken Kent to the possibilities for his petting zoo, hosting a birthday party here on the ranch was the perfect way to show him the place in a new light. Maybe then he'd reconsider his animal sanctuary.

"Maybe I shouldn't ask him. Kent doesn't socialize much anymore. He's all work," Carissa said.

"Maybe having people here again would help him socialize," Jaclyn said. "It can't hurt to ask."

"Casey would love riding the horses. I'm going to do it." Carissa wiped a tear from the corner of her eye then hugged Jaclyn. "Thank you."

Those words felt like an affirmation from heaven. Deeply moved, Jaclyn hugged back.

"What's going on in here?" Heddy demanded. "Is something wrong?"

"Everything's wonderful." Carissa patted Heddy's shoulder then walked out the kitchen door to talk to Kent.

"Is the cleaning finished in here?" Heddy asked.

"Just about." Amanda pointed to the counter. "We need to get those dishes back to folks before they leave."

Jaclyn grabbed an armful of the serving dishes and followed the others outside. She saw Heddy pick up a beautifully decorated casserole carrier.

"Is that yours?" she asked. When the older woman nodded, she said, "Would you mind telling me where you got it? It's lovely. The decoration is so intricate."

"I made it." Heddy smiled, obviously pleased by the compliment.

"She made that picture that hangs over the guest book at church, too," Amanda said. "And the runner that's on the communion table."

"I wish I knew how to create things like that." Jaclyn studied the woman with new eyes.

"I can show you." Heddy grinned. "You already know how to stitch people up. Stitching pictures isn't that much different."

"I'd like to learn," Jaclyn said.

"The question is when do you have free time? You're always on the go, rushing from one meeting to the next. Not that we aren't all grateful." Heddy stopped speaking when Kent appeared and touched Jaclyn on the arm.

"Can I speak to you privately?" he asked.

"Sure." Jaclyn followed him to an area away from the others.

"What are you doing?"

She blinked at his anger.

"Carissa said you volunteered my ranch for her daughter's party." His eyes shot angry sparks. "I'm up to my ears with your clinic. I can't take time off to host a birthday party and a bunch of kids."

"You need a break. Doctor's orders," she said as lightly as she could.

"You're a children's doctor," he snapped.

"And you're tired and overworked. Carissa will handle the food."

"And what will you do?"

"Me?"

"Yeah, you." A smirk kicked up the corners of his mouth. "Your suggestion, your party."

"But I don't know how to—"

"I'm sure you can figure it out," Kent said.

"This sounds like railroading," Jaclyn complained.

"Is it working?" His grin widened.

"Maybe." She huffed a sigh of resignation. "All right, let's do it together."

"The whole thing," Kent emphasized.

"Till the bitter end. I'll even stay late to help with cleanup." She raised one eyebrow. "Satisfied?"

"It's a start," he said, his electric blue eyes gleaming in a way that made her stomach do a little flip.

When Jaclyn's beeper went off, she excused herself, happy for a reason to put some distance between her and Kent Mc-Cloy.

The emergency she'd been beeped for turned out to be a sprain and took only a few minutes to treat, but Jaclyn stayed at the hospital. She needed to think through this party she suddenly found herself throwing.

"Bright colors," she murmured to herself, scribbling a list. "A few balloons in the kitchen would look like we'd brought the party indoors." She thought of that forlorn room and the equipment that begged to be used and enjoyed. "Red balloons, a few red dish towels, maybe a couple of red spoons and spatulas to go in that round utensil container."

Her brain echoed with Kent's laughter when Emma had giggled at the horses' whinnies. She remembered the patience and incredible softness today on Kent's handsome face as he held a new kitten so the children could see and touch. He'd let the littlest tots take turns holding tiny chicks he was keeping in a hen house. For those few moments this afternoon she knew he hadn't felt anything but pure joy.

You're supposed to be staying away from him.

"How can I?" she asked aloud as she drove home. "He's got a wonderful dream for that ranch and he's afraid to pursue it."

Jaclyn wanted to believe that she could help Kent make his dreams live without getting knocked off her own course, that she could help him realize his own personal dreams and not just those of the town of Hope.

"Maybe if I could understand why Kent's afraid to let go of the past then I'd know how best to help him."

Why does it matter so much? She avoided answering that by unlocking the door and rushing to answer the phone.

"Hi, Dad. What's up?"

"Your mother and I hoped maybe you'd changed your mind about the clinic and decided to forsake that horrible town and set up your practice in the city."

Where you can make a lot of money and be a success. Jaclyn heard the unsaid words.

"Your last email sounded as if there'd been nothing but problems."

"Oh, there are some issues, but we're working past them," she said, forcing cheeriness.

"And your lack of patients?"

Why had she ever confided that information? She constantly had to defend her decision to move here as it was. She didn't need to give her parents more ammunition to argue that she was making a mistake. Again.

"Jaclyn?" Her father's sharp voice cut off her introspection.

"I'm here. How are you and Mom?"

"Your mother is out right now. I'm going golfing. We were supposed to be planning our cruise to Iceland. It leaves in a little over a month."

"You won't be here for the opening of the clinic." Jaclyn struggled to mask her disappointment. "That's too bad. I wanted to show it to you."

"We told you we would never return to Hope." Her father's solemn voice echoed with pain. "Too many sad memories."

"Seeing the clinic might help erase some of them," Jaclyn said. Then it dawned on her that her parents' refusal probably had to do with her. They were ashamed and embarrassed by what she'd done, and what she was doing now hadn't changed anything.

"I have to go now. Tee time. I think your mother is having guests for dinner. She keeps quite busy with her friends." Disappointment lay buried in the words.

"I'm sorry I haven't emailed much. I'm on several committees and the time drain is enormous. But I want people here to see that I intend to be a full participant in town life."

"Does that matter?" her father asked. "You're there to treat their kids, aren't you? Not to make friends."

"Friends don't hurt," she replied, knowing there was no point in arguing it all again. "Have a good game, Dad. I love you."

"Let me know if you come to your senses and decide to join Dr. Hanson's practice. He's been asking after you."

"Bye, Dad." Jaclyn hung up, trying to shed a deep sense of discontent.

Her parents' lack of support for her clinic, despite it being named for Jessica, left Jaclyn aching and feeling empty. Then she glanced at her list for the birthday party.

"Maybe this is how Kent feels when he goes into that kitchen," she muttered to herself. "I have to do something." She poured a glass of iced tea, carried it out to her tiny patio and began to plan all the ways she could change Kent's world. Maybe she couldn't help her parents recapture the love they'd once had, but maybe she could help Kent find a new perspective on the world. Friends did that for each other.

Friend. Was that all Kent could be?

The day of the party dawned bright and sunny. Jaclyn rushed to prepare, pulling out the shopping bag she'd filled the evening before. She laid everything out on the table. Then the doorbell rang.

"Am I bothering you?" Heddy demanded.

"Not at all. Come in. I've just made a fresh pot of coffee." Jaclyn led the way to the kitchen. She reached out to scoop her purchases back into the bag.

"What's all this?" Heddy asked.

"Just some things I bought for Casey's party." Her face grew warm at Heddy's knowing look. "When we were there on Sunday I thought the kitchen could use some color. It must be hard for Kent to keep coming back into that stark room." She was babbling. "It was just an idea."

"A very kind one." Heddy accepted the coffee. "I must confess I've never given Kent's kitchen much thought. Except that it's useful for things like the potluck on Sunday and your birthday idea. I approve."

"Really?" Jaclyn sat down across from her. "I've been regretting that idea. Kent's always going out of his way for everyone. He does so much for the town and he's trying to get the clinic up and running. What am I adding to his load by suggesting he host a birthday party? It's presumptuous."

"On the contrary," Heddy reassured her. "Most of us in Hope take Kent for granted. He's the kind of mayor every town should have. He's caring, committed and he doesn't mind challenging us. But it's only since you came, Jaclyn, that I've started to wonder how many times he's put his life on hold for something we needed."

"I'm sure he took the job because he loves Hope and its people." Jaclyn glanced at the clock. Heddy was clearly bothered by something—she could hardly just hurry her on her way.

"His parents were so thrilled to adopt him. Mary once told me Kent was everything a son should be." Heddy stared into the distance. "When they moved to the ranch Kent was little. He was so polite, so quiet. Stan and Mary had to coax a smile. They found out later he was worried they'd send him away."

"I've known Kent since I moved here in junior high." Jaclyn shook her head in disbelief. "I never knew he was adopted."

"No, you wouldn't have. Stan and Mary didn't talk about it. Kent never does," Heddy told her. "He was their child. Period. He idolized them. Mary once told me Kent almost didn't take his vet's training."

"Why?" Kent had never talked of anything but veterinary training when they were in high school.

"Apparently Stan tended to go on and on about the ranch being his legacy. Kent felt that leaving would let down his father. I supposed he felt indebted. He even tried to hide his college acceptance but our postmistress knew every piece of mail that came into town and she clued Mary in. Mary read Kent the riot act and Kent went off to college. Then he married Lisa. Everything was wonderful until Stan and Mary died."

"And then Kent came back." Given this new perspective, Jaclyn now better understood Kent's reluctance to get rid of his father's cattle.

Heddy's round face filled with sadness. "After Lisa died, Kent was like a walking ghost. He just existed."

"So how did he become mayor?" Jaclyn asked.

"A child was hit running across Main Street. Kent happened on the scene moments later. When the stop signs he lobbied council for didn't happen, he ran for mayor. Got in by acclamation."

"And his mission to help Hope began." Jaclyn understood. Kent put aside his own dreams because he felt they weren't important. Somehow she had to show him that was not true.

"Heddy, don't be offended but I have to cut our coffee time short." Jaclyn smiled to soften the words. "I have some things to prepare for the party."

"I'm not offended." Heddy rose, dumped the rest of her coffee in the sink and stored her cup in the dishwasher. "Will you be offended if I purchase some materials to get you started on your needlework project?"

"No, but the truth is, Heddy, I don't know where I'll find the time to do needlework. I want to do it," she reassured. "But I'm so busy."

"You are. Sort of like Kent. Running around trying to make everyone else happy." Heddy leaned near, her voice very soft. "I often wonder when the two of you find time to lean on God and hear His direction. Nobody can fix all the world's ills, Jaclyn. Not even a wonderful doctor like you."

She patted Jaclyn's shoulder then let herself out.

Jaclyn considered her words. She wasn't being frivolous; she had a purpose in joining so many things. She already had a few new clients because people were beginning to get to know her. But to make Jessica's clinic viable, Jaclyn needed many more patients.

Jessica's clinic had to succeed, even if her parents didn't believe it would. Even if it meant she got only a few hours of sleep per night.

Yawning, Jaclyn grabbed the bag and headed for the door.

Today she'd try to help Kent. But after this party she'd draw the line between them. He was a business associate and that's all he could be, regardless of her silly heart. Her focus had to be on the clinic. Letting her emotions get control of her would only derail her goal.

Jaclyn was determined not to let that happen.

Chapter Eight

"Thank you, God, for sunshine."

Kent took a few moments to pray as he savored his coffee at sunrise. At least he called it praying. The gap between him and heaven had never seemed wider, nor had he ever felt more alone.

In a few hours the children would be here. He'd spent last evening mowing the yard and weeding the flower beds. He had groomed the animals, too, figuring that if they ran out of games, the children might like to see them.

Everything was ready.

She would be here.

Kent had pushed away thoughts of Jaclyn ever since the church potluck last weekend. He'd avoided her all week after insisting she be at the birthday party out of frustration that she'd volunteered his ranch. The potluck had been a special favor to the pastor, but this party—Kent sighed and admitted the truth.

He'd been avoiding her because he was embarrassed he'd revealed his stupid childish dream. He'd long ago accepted that animal sanctuaries and petting zoos were not going to be his lot in life. So why were those dreams still hanging around in the periphery of his mind?

Because they made the shambles of his life tolerable.

Behind him, someone coughed.

"Hey, Boss. I'm moving the herd higher up into the hills today. We're overgrazing on the lower levels. We might as well take advantage of the grass and water that's sitting up there free. It'll be gone once the heat hits." Gordon, his ranch manager, scuffed his toe against the pea gravel path.

Kent's dad had hired Gordon when he bought the ranch because of his vast knowledge. The herd had almost doubled since Stan's death. Several times the handyman had said the longhorns needed more grazing land than made up the ranch, but Kent ignored it because he didn't have the funds to expand and he couldn't bring himself to sell off his dad's prized animals.

"Okay." When Gordon didn't move, Kent frowned. "Something else on your mind?"

"I bought that land up against your southwest quarter. The price was right." Gordon coughed. "If you want to cut down on your herd, I'd sure like to buy some. Me and Stan talked a lot about when the herd got big. I have an itch to try out some of his ideas. He had some good plans."

And you—his son, his heir—don't.

Gordon knew more about the ranch than Kent. He certainly knew more about the animals. But the dream had been his dad's and Kent couldn't just sell it out.

"I'm not looking to sell any stock, Gordon."

"I know you're not ready yet. Thought if and when the time comes, you'd know I'm interested." He clamped his Stetson back on his head. "Time to git." He turned.

"Gordon?" Kent rose. "If I'm ever ready to sell Dad's herd, you'll be the first one I talk to, I promise. And congratulations on your land."

"Thanks." They shook hands.

Kent watched the older man walk away realizing Gordon

might one day leave here to run his own herd. For a few moments Kent imagined the ranch without the longhorns. Surprised by a sudden giddiness, he let the feeling linger until reality returned. He owed his father, for not being the son Stan expected.

"I aim to make the McCloy name the top one when it comes to longhorns." Kent could still hear the pride in those words. *"I love the law, but it takes second place when you look out the window and see your own cattle multiplying. Someday you'll feel the same, son."*

Only Kent never had felt that way about his father's beloved cattle.

"Good morning."

He turned and gulped at the beauty before him.

"Bad time?" Jaclyn paused, a frown marring the smoothness of her pale forehead. "Should I go and come again?"

"Of course not. I was just—" He didn't finish, mesmerized by the sight of her. She reached into her car. Out came bags and bags of things. "Must be planning a whale of a party." He moved forward to take them from her.

"I hope so." She wrestled out a bunch of colorful balloons and grinned at him. "Isn't it a lovely day?"

"Yeah." Lovely now, especially. Her smile turned him into a blithering idiot. And he liked it. "Where do you want these?" he asked, juggling his load.

"The kitchen." She followed him, her jumble of balloons bumping him in the back.

"Is there anything I can help with?"

"As a matter of fact, yes." She instructed him to tie balloons all around the yard. "And we'll need a table out here. Actually two."

There was nothing in Jaclyn's voice to suggest she was still angry at him for trying to tell her how to treat Joey or for conscripting her into this party, but Kent felt that the doctor was maintaining a barrier between them. His fault.

"Jaclyn, can I talk to you a minute?"

"Sure." She looked at him, poker-faced.

"I want to apologize again for asking you to back off Joey. It wasn't my call and I shouldn't have done it. I'm sorry."

"No problem." She turned away and continued fastening little curly ribbons to lawn chairs, planters, everything.

"That's it?" He'd expected something more.

"I don't hold grudges, Kent." Jaclyn straightened and faced him. "Besides, I finally realized that this thing you have about protecting everyone and everything in Hope was at the root of your meddling. You want the best for everyone and I threatened that so you stood up to me." She shrugged. "When you get to know me better you'll realize that the way you feel about Hope is the way I feel about my patients. Nothing will stop me from helping a child."

He gulped down his surprise that she was willing to let it go so easily.

"Now, let's focus on the party. We're going to need some benches by those tables."

The minute he filled one request, she found another, darting in and out of the house with stuff like a bird feathering its nest. By the time Carissa arrived with a van load of kids, his yard looked like party central.

"Everything is so pretty." Casey enveloped her pediatrician in a hug. She did the same to Kent. "This is the best birthday ever."

Kent watched as Casey opened her gift from Jaclyn. Soon the kids were chasing iridescent bubbles Casey was creating from a weird arrangement of pipes and hoops. The freshening breeze picked up the shimmering circles and tossed them around the yard.

"Great gift," he told her.

"Thanks." She slid sunglasses over her eyes. "What did you get for her?"

Kent grinned. "You'll see. Later."

Kent had been planning to disappear but both Carissa and Jaclyn insisted they needed a hand. The sound of children's squeals and giggles made the whole courtyard come alive with laughter. This was how he'd thought the ranch would one day sound when he'd first moved back here. He became so caught up in their joy, he blinked in surprise when a raindrop plopped onto his nose.

A moment later jagged lightning pierced the sky.

"I'm sorry, Kent." Jaclyn watched Carissa shepherd the children into the kitchen. "We'll have to hold the rest of the party inside." She grimaced. "When I suggested the ranch, I never meant we'd all be inside your house."

"It's not a problem." Kent hurried Jaclyn. The kids' laughter was gone. Big eyes brimmed with fear as another spear of lightening pierced the sky, its boom following a few seconds later. The festive party atmosphere had evaporated. Nobody was celebrating now. Except Jaclyn.

She handed everyone a red hat.

Kent blinked. Red pot mitts dangled from the oven door. There were red-and-white striped towels on the counter and two big white dishes with red polka dots that held what looked like party favor bags. Jaclyn struggled to fasten a Happy Birthday banner across the stainless-steel range hood. When he lent a hand, she smiled.

"You don't mind?"

"No." It was true. He didn't mind the extra touches, including the cherry-red pitcher on the counter and matching glasses. The room looked like a kitchen should—friendly, warm and welcoming. "I'll light a fire to take the chill off," he told her and soon had flames licking up the dry tinder and twigs in the adjoining eating area.

"We need some balloons for the last game." Jaclyn frowned. "Anyone interested in running outside to get them?" she asked loudly.

"Not me," the kids yelled en masse.

Jaclyn winked at him. "Anyone?" she said.

"Jaclyn, we don't need another game. Kent's done enough just letting us use his place." Carissa protested.

"I'll go," he volunteered. He raced outside to gather three bunches of balloons. Raindrops spattered his shirt, falling faster as the storm approached. He shoved the balloons into Jaclyn's arm and panted, "Gotta get the gifts," before returning to rescue the brightly colored packages and bags they'd forgotten.

When he had retrieved the last of them, he turned to leave the kitchen again.

"Kent, you don't need to get anything else," Jaclyn said quietly. "You'll get soaked."

"I'll be back in a few minutes," he promised.

"But you'll miss watching Casey open her gifts."

Kent lifted a hand to acknowledge he'd heard, but kept going. Inside his tool shed, he shook off the rain and fought to block out Jaclyn's effect on him. But he couldn't forget the image of her dashing across the grass in bare feet to avoid becoming "it" in a game of tag. He couldn't stop hearing the warming sound of her laughter when she'd been seriously splashed by a water gun. Nor could he rid his mind of the memory of her comforting a girl who'd slipped and skinned a knee.

Jaclyn pitched in whenever help was needed. Surely Hope-ites would soon not only accept her, but embrace her. Why, even Heddy had phoned this morning and apologized for asking him to intervene on Joey's behalf.

Kent hurried back to the house, surprised by his eagerness to rejoin the festivities. For so long he'd kept on the fringes of

life, but Jaclyn and this silly party were reawakening feelings
he'd thought long dead. It was dangerous to get involved—
but suddenly Kent didn't care.

He left his box on the porch and went inside. Satisfaction
filled him at the sight of kids gathered round the fireplace,
laughing and talking as Casey opened the last of her gifts.
The room was messy and happy and full of life.

Kent waited until Casey had finished thanking her friends
for her birthday gifts. Then he carried in his and set it down
in front of her.

"This is for you. Happy Birthday."

Casey's eyes gaped. She froze for a minute in disbelief,
then reached out one finger and touched Kent's surprise.

"A puppy! Oh, Mommy, it's a puppy." She hugged the furry
little body to her chest and burbled with laughter when a tiny
pink tongue peeked out to lick her face. "Can I really keep it?"

"Yes, Casey. Kent asked me and I agreed that you could
have it. But you're going to have to take care of it. A puppy
is a big responsibility." Carissa smiled at him.

Jaclyn's gaze held admiration. *Life is good,* Kent thought,
basking in the warmth of her smile.

"I promise I will take very good care of him." Casey put
the dog down and let it walk around the circle of kids, sniffing as it went. "What's his name, Mr. Kent?"

"Her, and the name is for you to decide." He glanced at
Carissa. "As soon as you've chosen a name, I'll register her.
She's a purebred Springer spaniel so you might as well have
the papers."

"It's very kind of you, Kent. I know you usually sell your
dogs. I appreciate you trusting Casey with one." Tears sparkled on the tips of Carissa's lashes as she watched her daughter roll on the floor with the puppy.

"What are you going to call her, Casey?" Jaclyn asked.

Casey thought for a moment then declared, "Marjorie

Rose, that's her name. Only sometimes I'll call her Marj. Or maybe Rosie."

The dog had been well admired by the time Carissa called the children to the table. Kent intervened before Casey could feed Marjorie tidbits and explained the dog could have only puppy food.

"You mean she can't have any birthday cake?" Casey wailed.

"No." He hunkered down next to her. "Marjorie Rose can never have treats like yours. They will make her sick. You don't want to hurt her, do you?"

"No." Casey was adamant. She'd been sick so long that she had no desire to inflict that on anyone or anything else. "But what can she eat?"

"Her own food. And once in a while doggie treats." He pulled a sample from his pocket, winked at Jaclyn then set the treat on the floor. The dog careened over to it in a crazy bumbling scramble, wolfed down the biscuit then sneezed.

The kids erupted into roars of laughter.

"Oh, Marjorie, you need some manners." Casey's rapt adoration turned on Kent. "Thank you very much, Mr. Kent."

"You're welcome, honey. Just take care of her."

"I will." Casey cuddled the puppy under one arm.

Kent sat in the corner next to a bemused Oreo, content to watch as Jaclyn helped Carissa serve the usual birthday fare. Cooking in this kitchen always made him feel like he was ruining Lisa's perfection. Today he'd seen how the room should feel and sound. It was not a memory he'd quickly forget.

The cake appeared, candles glowing. Kent joined in the singing when Jaclyn shot him a look. Then he savored every bite of the delicious chocolate cake.

"Seconds?" Jaclyn asked.

"I'd better not. I'm like Marjorie Rose—too many sweets aren't good for me."

"Oh, live a little," Jaclyn urged and plopped an oversize section on his plate. "I'll do CPR if you have cardiac arrest."

"Do I look like I'll have a heart attack?" He was indignant at the suggestion.

"You make it so easy," she teased.

"The sun is shining again," Carissa said. "Why don't we take Marjorie Rose outside and you kids can play with her?"

Kent could have pointed out that the dog would get dirty and have to be bathed. But instead, he followed the ladies outside, sat in one of his mom's favorite lawn chairs and enjoyed the laughter of the kids—almost as much as he enjoyed his second piece of cake.

"This has been such a lovely day. Thank you, Kent." Carissa's eyes grew moist. "Casey will never forget this birthday."

"Glad to help," he said, smiling.

Casey wasn't the only one who wouldn't forget today.

Suddenly Kent jumped out of his chair and raced across the grass as fear clamped a hand around his heart. One of the kids had used his barbecue lighter to set fire to some twigs.

"Kent?" Jaclyn said from behind him. He turned and she glanced from the lighter to his face, and took over. "That's really dangerous, honey," she told the child. "Fire can spread very easily when it's so dry. Then it's hard to put out."

"But it was just raining," the little girl protested.

"It didn't rain much. The ground isn't even muddy. The sun has dried it all up." She ran her fingers over the ground to show the dust. "See? Fire is not for playing."

"Okay." She shrugged and rejoined the rest of the kids.

"Come on, Kent," Jaclyn soothed as she took his arm. "Have another cup of coffee. Everything is fine."

"Fine?" He turned on her, yanking his arm from her grasp. "That child could have been hurt and it would have been my fault."

"Kids get into mischief. Nothing happened." She'd turned

her back so the others couldn't see, her voice soft. "God gave us a lovely day and kept us safe. Let's enjoy it."

God kept them safe? Then why hadn't God protected Lisa?

"Nothing happened, Kent."

But Kent knew exactly how quickly things could change.

Casey's party was the first and last that would ever happen on his ranch.

No matter what Jaclyn wanted.

Chapter Nine

"This is the last of them." Kent set a tray of used dishes on the counter in the kitchen. "You don't have to do this, Jaclyn. My housekeeper will clean it up tomorrow morning."

"We're not leaving this for her." She kept working.

He gave a long-suffering sigh. "How can I help?"

"I can manage."

"I know that, Doc. By now I expect everyone in Hope knows exactly how well you manage to do anything you set your mind to." He grasped her shoulders and turned her to face him. "But since I'm here, we'll do it together. Deal?"

She nodded as she shrugged out of his hold. "Deal." Maybe working would take her mind off what had happened with the child and the lighter, and the strong urge she'd had to help Kent in that moment.

While she loaded the dishwasher, he wiped down counters, tables and chairs.

"Sorry I got so upset earlier," he finally said. "I just saw that flame flickering and—"

"You remembered the fire and Lisa," she finished. She fought not to look at him lest she be bowled over by his pain. "I guessed that's what happened. It's only natural. After all, you haven't had a lot of people around since the accident, have you? Except for the potluck."

His blue eyes met hers. "You don't have to save my feelings, Jaclyn. I know I went over the top. But I couldn't stand it if a child got hurt out here."

She set the now-clean red utensils in the stainless-steel bucket on the counter then turned to face him.

"You think someone would blame you? Accidents happen, Kent. To everyone. We pick up and move on as best we can, but we can't always prevent them."

He raked his hand through his hair, sending the dark curls into further disarray. "It's so terribly dry," he mumbled, staring out the window.

"That's in God's hands. Not yours."

"Well, it's partly in my hands." He looked away from her and fell into a brooding silence.

"What's bothering you?" She sat down at the table and waited. "Talk to me, Kent. Is it about your cattle?"

"My cattle?" He frowned, his gaze confused as he studied her.

"I've been thinking about what you said about them. Can you not sell because cattle prices are low right now?"

"Not exactly." He tapped his finger on the table.

"Then what?" She searched her mind for memories of his dad. "You said your father understood about you not wanting to stay on the ranch after high school."

"He did."

"Then why would he expect you to keep his animals? I think he'd want you to be happy." Nothing about Kent's reluctance made sense to her. "Wouldn't building a sanctuary make you happy?"

"Yes." His entire demeanor changed. "If I just had an area where the wild animals I treat could be free instead of confined to cages or stalls until I reintroduce them to the wild—" His voice drifted away.

"That sounds simple," she reasoned.

"It's far from simple." His tortured voice told her the struggle went way beyond longhorn cattle.

"Because?" Jaclyn said softly.

"Because I owe my father." Desperation laced his voice. "I owe a lot to Dad and Mom, and I want to honor that."

She kept silent, waiting for him to continue, hoping she'd finally get an inkling as to why he felt so strongly about this.

"They loved me when no one else did." Kent squeezed his eyes closed. "I'm adopted, Jaclyn. No one around here knows." He got up, poured them each a glass of the lemonade his housekeeper had made and carried it to the table. He sat down, drained his own glass, set it on the table and looked directly at her.

"Heddy told me that the other day." Jaclyn shook her head before he could ask. "I haven't told anyone, but why is your adoption such a big secret?"

"My mom. She couldn't have children. She always felt bad about it. Embarrassed, I guess. Like she'd somehow let Dad down." A funny sad smile skittered across his lips. "It's understandable given how crazy the McCloys were about the heir and oldest son thing—a son to carry on the legacy. I broke the chain. I disappointed them."

"I doubt it."

"About a year after they officially adopted me, we moved here. My grandparents were gone. We had no other family. As far as I knew they never told anyone I was adopted." He shrugged. "That probably seems stupid to you."

"Not at all. I can understand wanting to keep private information to yourself, though I imagine it was hard on you."

"Me?" He blinked. "Why?"

"It's kind of denying a part of yourself, isn't it?" she asked.

"You kept that secret from us, your friends. You couldn't be open and honest about it."

"I didn't want to be honest about my birth mother abandoning me." His mouth tightened. "Being adopted was the best thing to happen to me in my life and I repaid that by denying Dad his dream. All those years he'd talked about passing on the ranch to me." Kent's voice caught. When he looked at her, his blue eyes brimmed with sadness. "But he didn't say a word to dissuade me. The morning after my announcement he was talking funding for college. My father gave me my dream, Jaclyn. Now it's my turn to make his dream live."

"Kent." She reached out and laid her hand on his, waiting until he looked at her. "Cattle, longhorns—I doubt that's what your father dreamed of for you."

"It was all he ever talked about." He stared at their hands and then entwined his fingers with hers.

"Maybe all he talked of to you. To everyone else it was 'My son this and my son that.'" She smiled. "I talked to my dad the other evening. I told him you were mayor, and about all the things you're doing to improve the town. Do you know what he said?"

Kent shook his head.

"He said, 'Stan would be really proud of that boy. He used to say God brought the McCloys to Hope to make a difference. Kent is certainly doing that.'" She squeezed his fingers "That was your father's dream, Kent. Not those cattle—they were just a game he played. You were what mattered to him, you and your integrity, the way you live your life. He taught you those things, didn't he?"

Kent nodded. "Yeah." His eyes glazed with memories. "Yes, he did."

"Maybe at first he was disappointed you didn't share his plans for the ranch. But once he saw the way you are with animals?" She shook her head. "I believe your dad wanted you to use that special gift you have and that's why he made it easy for you to get to college."

He bent his head to stare at their hands.

"Talk to anyone downtown, Kent. Go for coffee and ask them about your father. I guarantee every single person who knew him will tell you that next to you, those cattle came a distant second." She smiled at him as another memory surfaced. "We used to be in awe of you and your parents, did you know that? The rest of us kids used to wish we were that close with our parents."

"Yeah, we were pretty close. Dad used to say we were each other's cheering section and backup team." He closed his eyes.

"Exactly." Jaclyn cleared her throat. "Now are you going to live up to his dreams—his real ones—or are you going to get sidetracked?"

She could sit here and watch him forever, she thought, but handsome was only part of Kent's allure. He was strong, caring and determined to help everyone else. Here he was, ready to sacrifice his own dreams, as if they weren't worth the same effort he put into helping Hope.

"How do you do it?" Kent asked when she'd sipped the last drop from her glass.

"Do what?"

"Find exactly the right words to say." He leaned forward, brushed a strand of hair from her brow and peered into her eyes. "How did you know how to help me see what my dad was really about?"

She felt dazed by his touch. "Is that what I've done?"

He nodded, his face solemn.

"Well, maybe it's because I believe God has a purpose for each of us. You already know what I think mine is." She smiled. "Jessica's clinic."

"Like I needed to be told that."

"What you need to be told is, figure out your own purpose, Kent. I've watched you with kids, animals, the people of Hope—you really care about them. You go out of your way to make their worlds better. That is what your dad taught you. That is his real legacy to you. Not the cattle."

"See? You're so smart." He leaned forward and brushed her nose with a kiss. "Are you starving?"

Her insides melted at the kiss, innocent though it had been.

"How can you possibly be starving? You just ate a ton of cake," she said, trying to pretend she'd barely felt a thing.

"It was delicious, but it was *just* cake." He jumped up, strode to the fridge and peered inside. "Interested in a steak dinner, Doc? I'm cooking."

"Really?" She leaned back to study him. "I didn't realize you cooked."

"Actually I grill." Kent grinned. "Want to see?"

Jaclyn walked outside with him, marveling at the naturalness of his arm slung across her shoulders. He didn't seem to notice she was short of breath. She tried to ignore the warning bells going off in her head.

"Well?" He stood before a huge stainless-steel outfit built into an outdoor kitchen which Jaclyn was pretty sure would make most men drool. "What do you think?"

"That is not a grill. That is restaurant equipment." She had to step away from him in order to keep her thoughts together.

"My own personal restaurant. I'm pretty good with this." He picked up a lifter and twirled it like a juggler, tossing it up then catching it with two fingers.

"Do I applaud now?"

"Not till after you eat." Kent headed back into the house and began rummaging in the fridge.

Jaclyn stayed on the patio and searched for order in her chaotic thoughts. She was supposed to be avoiding him, but, oh, she wanted to stay and share a meal, to talk as they had been, open and honestly.

I have my work. I have the clinic. I have the committees. I don't have time for Kent or any other man in my life.

The thing was, Kent was already in her life.

For so long she'd defined herself as a doctor, indebted to God and her parents, a single twin. Was it time to rework her definition?

"You're not waiting to be served, are you?" Kent burst through the door bearing a huge platter with two steaks that flopped over the edges. "Because I was hoping you'd make a salad or something." He paused in front of her and bent to look into her eyes, one brow arched upward in an unasked question. "What's wrong?" he finally said.

"Nothing." She smiled. "I'd love to make a salad. That's one area in which I excel." She stepped inside.

A minute later she heard him humming a new song they'd learned in church last week. Jaclyn smiled as she moved around the kitchen, finding what she needed to set the table on the patio. She made tea, put two scrubbed potatoes in the microwave and threw together a salad. In the freezer there was half a loaf of garlic bread which she wrapped in foil and placed in the oven on low to heat. As she worked, Jaclyn realized the kitchen was perfectly planned out to facilitate every task. Nothing was more than a few steps away.

Just beyond the window over the sink, red roses bloomed in profusion, adding another touch of color to the room. With a few lights on and the new accessories, the kitchen looked, almost welcoming.

Some shrunken apples lay in a crisper in the fridge. She peeled them, added cinnamon and placed them in the oven beside the bread.

"Something smells good in here." Kent glanced around. "How rare do you like your steak?" His big grin made him look relaxed and happy.

"Not at all. This is to say—well done." She quickly dissolved into giggles at his offended look. "I know, it's the wrong thing to say to a rancher, but it's true. Make it well done, please."

"You mean ruin it." His face morose, Kent returned to his grill.

As she tidied up, Jaclyn found an old candle stub in a drawer. But when she lit it, it made everything feel too intimate. She was about to blow it out when Kent set two huge plates on the table.

"Enjoy," he said with a flourishing bow.

And she did. The food, the laughter, the teasing and the unfamiliar pleasure of eating with someone you liked—it made her realize how isolated she'd been. The talk soon turned to some mutual high school friends.

"I think Brianna, Zac, Nick, Shay, you and I are the only ones who aren't married." Jaclyn regretted the words the moment she said them. "I mean, you were, of course. But—"

"It's okay. I know what you mean." He patted her hand. "But I don't think it's all that odd. You, Brianna and Shay were pretty career-minded. It's hard to have it all." He pushed away his dish, leaned back in his chair. "I should know."

"What does that mean?" Night edged in around them and the rose bush filled the air with its intoxicating scent. "Is fixing the clinic getting to you?" she asked softly.

"Only because I can't seem to get it done." He sighed.

"And you want to? You're sure?"

"Of course I want you to get in there, to have a real office. I want your patients lined up and waiting because I happen to think you have a lot to give this town." He grimaced. "But that isn't exactly what I meant."

"What did you mean?" She never tired of the smooth, even cadence of his voice.

"There are so many things Hope needs and it's up to me to get them done. People are counting on me. I can't fail them."

"I'm sure no one feels you have failed them," she protested.

"I feel it." He looked straight at her, his blue eyes unflinching. "I have a list of things I want to accomplish before my term is up and—don't take this personally—but it's about as long as it was two months ago."

She frowned, intrigued by his comment. "What kinds of things?"

"Redoing the baseball diamond so it doesn't look like our little league kids have been abandoned to a vacant lot, refinishing the stucco on the outside of the hospital, starting some kind of youth program so our kids have a place to go after school and in the evenings."

"All of them sound achievable to me," she said.

"Mostly I'd like to formulate an emergency measures plan." His face tightened. A furrow formed between his brows. "If we have another wildfire, if the mine has a major incident, or if anything else disastrous happens, Hope is totally unprepared."

"I thought I saw something about that when I signed on at the hospital," Jaclyn said.

"There was a plan developed about thirty-five years ago but things have changed since then. We need to update, to be prepared in case some kind of disaster hits." Kent fell silent, his face bearing that worried expression.

"You're expecting problems?" she asked quietly.

"I'm expecting the unexpected because that's what usually happens when you're not prepared." A taut grimness edged his tone now.

"We'll have to pray that won't happen." She saw his eyes narrow.

"Pray, yes. But I also want to be organized for whatever gets thrown at us. With such a dry year—" His voice trailed away, his eyes peering into the darkness.

"You're worried about another fire. It could happen, I suppose. I've noticed areas around the hospital are very dry." She tried to ease his worry. "But whatever comes our way, God will take care of us. That's His promise. We can always depend on Him."

Jaclyn knew he didn't believe it. He was thinking about Lisa and the fire that had taken her. Was that why he sounded so driven when he talked about the emergency preparedness plan?

"I still think we need to get all our ducks in a row, just in case," he muttered.

"It's a good idea," she agreed. "If you want some help, let me know. I'd like to be part of it."

"Thanks." Kent nodded then rose and began stacking their dishes.

Jaclyn took the cue, but his response bothered her. Didn't he want her help?

"It's getting late. I'll help you clean up then I'd better go. I'm on call tonight."

"Then you shouldn't be here working. You should be relaxing." He took the dishes from her and insisted she leave them. "You've done enough for today. Go home, Jaclyn. Relax and do something special for yourself this evening."

"But—" The word spluttered out of her before she could stop it.

"But what?" He smiled. "I am capable of doing a few dishes you know."

"I know that." She debated whether or not to say it.

He gave her an odd look. "What?"

"I wanted to see your petting zoo."

"I don't have one." The familiar tic was back at the corner of his jaw, telegraphing his tension.

"You did show the kids something today—they told me. I wanted to see but I was busy attending to a bump on the head."

"The puppies. And I have a couple of birds I've worked on that are healing out in the shed. And one of the miniature ponies had a colt." He shrugged. "That's it. Oh, except for the snakes. The game wardens brought in a couple of snakes yesterday, but I only let the kids look at them."

"That's all?" Jaclyn mocked and burst into laughter. "It sounds like a regular petting zoo to me. One of the children mentioned a rabbit?"

"Yes," he agreed dryly. "There is also a rabbit, soon to be more rabbits if my diagnosis is correct. But that doesn't make a petting zoo."

"What would you call it then?" She tilted her head to one side.

"It's just a few animals that I'm treating. A petting zoo would have specific areas and pens designed for each animal." He shrugged. "I don't have any of that."

"Yet." She checked her watch. "I guess I'll have to see them another time." She grabbed her bag and slung it over one shoulder.

"It was the snakes that did it, wasn't it?" He grinned. "You were all ready to run out there and see the animals until I mentioned snakes."

Jaclyn tried and failed to hide her shudder.

"Snakes are amazing animals you know, even the poisonous ones." He chuckled at her. "You don't believe me?"

"I guess it's all in the way you look at things." She met his gaze. "Like I look at God as someone who expects each of us to do our very best for Him so we're worthy of the life He gives us."

"Really?" Kent frowned at her. "I guess I don't see Him the same as you do. I don't feel like He's a big taskmaster who expects me to accomplish certain things or He'll disapprove."

"I never said that at all."

"You act that way. Signing up for all these committees, working yourself to death—what is that about?"

"Hardly to death." She held out her arms, fingers splayed so he could see they were not worked to the bone. "See? Perfectly healthy. And you know why I joined all those committees. I am trying to get clients for the clinic."

"I know it's been hard to get patients," he said, modulating his voice. "I know lots of folks have brought up the past and made it their excuse for not coming to see you. But I don't think you have to earn anything. God gives us His gifts because He loves us, not because we earn them. People in Hope will eventually come around. People like you, Jaclyn."

"So far 'like' hasn't been working." She studied the floor. "I don't know if you can understand this. My parents certainly don't. But the clinic—that is what I'm supposed to do with my life. It's what I *have* to do. Otherwise what was the purpose for me living and Jessica dying?"

Kent stared at her. A frown tipped down the edges of his mouth and darkened his eyes to a deep navy. "You're trying to earn your life?" Disbelief filled his voice.

"Yes," she told him, thrusting back her shoulders and tilting up her chin so he wouldn't feel sorry for her. "That is exactly what I'm saying. God gives us opportunities. He expects us to make use of them. And if we don't—"

"If we don't—what?" he asked in disbelief.

"I'm not saying that God sends down a lightning rod to strike us dead if we don't use what He's given us." She drew her bag a little closer, trying to form the words. "But that doesn't mean God has no expectations of His children. There's an old saying. 'God helps those who help themselves.'"

Kent looked as if he wanted to argue. Jaclyn just wanted to escape. Suddenly she felt vulnerable, as if she'd opened up a private part of herself for him to examine and she'd disappointed him. She edged toward the door.

"Thank you for a lovely dinner. I don't know when I've tasted a better steak."

"I'm the one who needs to thank you," he said as he followed her outside. "You did so much work for that party."

"A party you didn't want. Anyway, Carissa did most of the work." She opened her car, set her bag inside. "I just helped."

"That's what you always do, isn't it? *Just* help. You help the girls' group, you help the ladies' committees. You help the Sunday school. You help the choir. You help the service clubs. In fact you 'help' pretty well everyone in town." Kent tipped his head to one side, his eyes quizzical in the clear moonlight. "It makes me wonder—who is helping you, Jaclyn?"

"You are," she said softly. Her nerves were doing that skittering dance again. Her pulse picked up when she caught the citrusy scent of his aftershave. Every nerve ending turned into a megawatt receptor that flashed details about Kent to her brain. "You're a wonderful man who has worked so hard to make my dream come true. I appreciate you, Kent. Good night."

He said nothing until she was seated in her car. Then he leaned inside and pressed a kiss against her cheek, right at the edge of her lips. A moment later he pulled back and closed the door. Jaclyn started the motor then rolled down the window.

"What was that for?" she asked, bemused.

"For bringing life back to this ranch," he said. "That's what you helped with today, Jaclyn. Good night."

Jaclyn had no recollection of driving home. As she stood in her own kitchen, she lifted her hand and touched her fingertips to spot beside her mouth that still burned from Kent's kiss.

"For a doctor, you're a very stupid woman, Jaclyn LaForge. You've gone and fallen in love with him."

Kent wasn't interested in a romantic relationship. He was still reeling from the loss of the wife he loved.

"I can't love him," Jaclyn whispered. Running the clinic would drain her, physically, emotionally and mentally. There wouldn't be enough left over to give to someone else. Besides, she didn't want marriage. She'd seen how badly marriage could go with her parents, who had truly loved each other once.

Jaclyn had known she'd be alone when she made the decision to make the clinic her life. She couldn't vacillate now.

She dug out her plans for Jessica's clinic and poured over them for hours. But always it was Kent's face she saw, his voice she heard, his kiss she felt. She wished an emergency would draw her to the hospital where she could dive into work and forget these very unsettling feelings.

Instead, Jaclyn sat far into the night, dreaming of what she couldn't have.

I'm trying to keep my vow, she prayed when sleep wouldn't come. *Please help me forget love and focus on work.*

But in her heart Jaclyn knew her work couldn't compete with what she now felt for Kent McCloy.

She was in trouble.

Chapter Ten

Two weeks later Kent sat in church wishing he'd skipped this Sunday service. It felt wrong to be here when the faith he'd once held so dear now filled him with questions. But he could hardly walk out just as the minister walked to the pulpit.

"What are you blaming God for?" he asked the congregation. "Is it a lack of money? A lousy boss? The loss of someone you loved? Do you think you're alone, that you've been abandoned? Do you feel like God is mad at you? What's your beef with God, folks?"

The pregnant pause had the entire church riveted, including Kent.

"You need help, but where is God? Where does He go when you need Him most? More importantly, why doesn't He help when you call? It's an age-old question. And the answer is—" Pastor Tom paused, waited then smiled. "I don't know."

Soft laughter filled the sanctuary.

"It's the truth, people. I don't know why it's that way. I don't know why it sometimes feels as if God abandons us. I can't explain why certain times in our lives we are unable to hear His voice or feel His presence." Again his smile flashed. "I do know we humans sometimes feel disappointed in His response. We think we have to work harder to get His attention, to be worthy of His time. And if God still doesn't respond, we feel abandoned, alone, as if we've sinned, done something so wrong He's finally given up on us."

Kent squirmed. This sermon hit a little too close to home.

"David the psalmist, God's chosen king and beloved child, had the same questions we do. Read his psalms and you'll see how often David asked God where He is, why He doesn't help. If David had doubts, why wouldn't we?" The pastor shook his head. "We have to stop beating ourselves up when doubts assail us. We need to remember who God said He is and the promises He's made. We have to stop allowing doubts and fears to overwhelm us. When problems hit us, when it seems we're at rock bottom, this is the very time we need to hold strong in our faith."

Uncomfortable with the message, Kent glanced around. He noticed Jaclyn seated two rows over in front of him. She wore a white lace sundress that showed off her narrow shoulders. On her left side, three young girls hunched forward, intent on the minister's words. Jaclyn also seemed riveted until she turned her head, as if she'd felt his stare on her. Her eyes met his and held as if some invisible electric current bound them together. After a moment she gave him a funny half smile, then turned her attention back to the preacher. Kent did the same.

"We all have dark moments when the questions seem to overwhelm. But in David's blackest hour, he knew enough about God to know His truth. Listen to Psalm 139, verse seven." He turned a page in his Bible and began to read. "'I can never be lost to your Spirit! I can never get away from my God! If I go up to heaven, You are there; if I go down to the place of the dead, You are there. If I ride the morning winds to the farthest oceans, even there Your hand will guide me, Your strength will support me.' And then in verse sixteen he says, 'You saw me before I was born and scheduled each day of my life before I began to breathe.'"

The magnitude of that hit Kent like a sledgehammer. Somehow he'd never considered that God had known him before he was born and knew how badly he would fail Lisa. He'd never considered that God knew, before Kent had packed a single bag, that coming back to the ranch would send his wife into that tailspin of depression.

He and Lisa had prayed before they moved. They'd asked God's blessing. Kent had done everything he could to ease the transition for her. And yet even then, God knew it wouldn't be enough.

Kent struggled with the truth that God had also known how Lisa would die and that the guilt of her death would bring Kent to the very precipice of doubting his faith. Shock filled him as he realized that long before he'd admitted it to himself, God had known his questions.

If Lisa's death had been a test of his faith, Kent had failed miserably.

Lost in his musing, he suddenly became aware that the congregation was rising, that the organ was playing. The service was over. He stood and scanned the overhead for the words to a chorus he didn't really know, his brain focused on clarifying the meaning of those scriptures.

God knew of his guilty feelings, of his failure of the one he loved the most. God knew Kent was immobilized by blame and remorse and shame. Because if he was honest with himself, that is what lay under his guilt—shame. Shame that he had not been able to save his wife. Shame that he hadn't loved her enough to take her away before it was too late.

Did that make Lisa's death any less his fault?

"Hi, Kent. I'm glad you made it this morning." Jaclyn stood in front of him, breathtaking in her white dress.

"You're glad?" Did that mean she'd noticed he'd skipped church lately?

"I went out on a call last night at eleven. When I came back at two, I noticed your truck was still in front of the clinic. You keep late hours." Her wide smile did funny things to his respiration.

"I guess you do, too. You look lovely. No one would know you were up so late." He searched for another topic of conversation. "Was it serious—the call, I mean?"

Jaclyn nodded, her face solemn. When she swallowed he saw the shadow of tears well in her brown eyes. That vulnerability sent a shaft of pain straight to his heart.

"A little boy, only two. I lost him," she murmured. "I did everything I could think of to save him, but they brought him in too late because they knew I was on duty." A tiny sob stopped her words for a moment.

"Oh, I'm so sorry, Jaclyn." He wanted to hug her.

"Thanks." She struggled to regroup. "I'm beginning to wonder if I will ever crack the barrier of trust in Hope," she whispered.

"Can you tell me who it was?" Kent was stunned when she named the child of a former school friend of theirs.

"The mom's parents never got over their bitterness about me. They advised their daughter to wait until another doctor came on duty." She dashed the tears from her cheeks and gulped. "Maybe if someone else had been—"

"No, don't think that. You can't blame yourself, Jaclyn." Kent touched her arm, her bare skin smooth against his work-roughened fingertips. "I know you. You did the best you could."

"Yes. I did everything I know to do." Jaclyn nodded. "But the pneumonia—"

"There are no buts." He smiled at her. "In a way, isn't that what today's message was about? Knowing that God is there, that we do the best we can and leave the rest up to Him. At least," he said, trying for a lighter tone, "that's my interpretation."

"I guess." Her face looked pale. "But this case has magnified my doubts. Maybe my parents were right and it's time for me to join a big-city practice." She drew her arm away from his touch then tilted her head to one side and said, "Maybe it would be better if someone else came here, someone they wouldn't be afraid to let treat their kids. Maybe Jessica's clinic was a selfish idea that I need to forget."

Kent stifled his urge to yell "no" at the top of his lungs. He wanted to beg her to stay, but then Jaclyn might suspect the depths of his feelings for her. He didn't want that, so he modified his response and tried another tack.

"That's a whole lot of maybes. I don't think you should give up just yet. I think this is something you need to seriously consider, not decide on the spur of the moment. I'm happy to act as your sounding board, if you want."

"That's really nice of you, Kent. I could use a friend."

He nodded, knowing his feelings were much stronger than friendship.

"Maybe you'd like to join me for lunch." Her hesitancy over the invitation transmitted clearly through her uncertain voice.

"Sure. Where would you like to go?"

"My place? I couldn't sleep when I got home so I tried out some recipes from my cooking class. I know it's a risk, but you could share them with me." She grimaced. "I promise I have a large bottle of antacids, in case you need them."

Though he had avoided Jaclyn this past week, sharing lunch with her sounded too good to resist. And he wanted to learn if she identified with what the minister had said.

"Kent," she said, giving a nervous laugh. "You're taking way too long to answer."

"Uh, I—"

"In my defense, I've had five classes now and turned out an acceptable dish for every one. Heddy's standing right over there. Ask her if you don't believe me."

Kent glanced around the sanctuary and saw Hope's busiest busybody studying them. He knew in a minute she would rush over to see if he'd made a decision about her offer to work on the emergency measure plan and he didn't want that. Not now. What he wanted was some time with Jaclyn. Alone.

Jaclyn, with her generous smile and infectious laugh was getting to be a big part of his formerly solitary life.

Too big a part?

"Another time," she said, a flicker of hurt in her voice. She shrugged, turned away. "See you."

Jaclyn had made it out the foyer door before Kent caught up to her.

"I'd be very happy to share whatever you prepared," he said. "I'm sure it's all delicious."

"It's not necessary, really. I got the message, Kent."

"That's funny because I wasn't sending any message. I admit I kind of zoned out there for a minute, but that had to do with Heddy." He grimaced. "Somehow she always manages to corner me and talk me into something I don't want to do. I was trying to think up a way to decline her latest request to be in charge of the emergency measures planning committee and I wasn't paying attention to you. Sorry."

"Heddy wants to be in charge—oh, dear."

"Exactly," he agreed. "If she was in charge a lot of people wouldn't help. I can't think of a way to refuse her."

Jaclyn studied him. "Okay, lunch it is. We could go out. You don't have to eat what I made." Her perfectly arched brows lowered. "It's probably not that good anyway."

"I won't be able to tell until I have some," he said. "I'll follow you to your place, shall I?"

The drive to Jaclyn's town home was short. Curiosity built as he trailed her up the path to her front door.

She unlocked it and invited him inside. Kent glanced around. It was more or less what he'd expected—very stylish, quite modern and extremely tidy.

"Your home is lovely," he said. "I would have known it was yours."

She laid her purse on the sofa then turned to look at him. "How?"

"The red," he said. "It's your signature color, I think. I notice you usually wear some touch of red, most of the time in the form of funny earrings."

"You think my earrings are funny?" Jaclyn began pulling dishes out of the fridge. "My patients like them."

"And it's the kids that count, right?" Kent grinned when she nodded. "I figured." He watched her remove lids, clear plastic wrap and tinfoil from a number of bowls. "How can I help?"

"Set the table?" Jaclyn waited for his nod then pointed to a drawer.

"What did you think of the sermon today?" He worked quickly as he waited for her answer, wondering if he'd overreacted to what he'd heard.

"Good. But then his sermons are always good." She set the last of the serving dishes on the table and waved him to a seat. "I like the way he makes God personal. I'll say grace."

Kent bowed his head and waited until she finished speaking, searching for a way to ask the questions that rattled in his brain.

"Now help yourself. Take a little bit first," she warned. "I haven't tasted this yet myself."

"It looks good." As he sampled each dish, he decided to come right out with it. "Can I ask you something?"

Jaclyn grinned at him. "As long as you don't ask me if I followed the recipe exactly."

"Recipe or not, it all tastes wonderful to me." He chewed on a biscuit until the silence had gone on too long and he knew he had to ask. "I was wondering about something you said when you were at my house. After the birthday party, remember?"

"I remember," she said cautiously, not looking at him. The way she kept her head bent, her eyes on her food, made him think she was remembering that kiss.

He'd been an idiot to do it, but he didn't regret it.

"You were saying?" Confusion filled her pretty face.

He cleared his throat. "I don't remember your exact words, but when we were talking it sounded to me like you felt that you owe God for allowing you to live." It wasn't exactly the way he meant to say it, but close enough. "Do you really think that?"

"Yes," she said thoughtfully. "I do feel I owe God, though perhaps not the way you mean it."

"Would you mind explaining how *you* mean it?"

"Well." Jaclyn set down her fork and leaned back in her chair. "Jessica and I were identical twins, yet she got sick and I didn't. I finished high school, I took my training and now I'm able to work, to enjoy life and to think about the future. That's a gift from God and I need to be worthy of it."

"How?" he asked. "How can you make yourself worthy of your life?" He took another spoonful of potato salad and a larger scoop of the green bean salad. "These are excellent by the way."

"Thanks." She rose and filled the electric kettle, then set it to boil. She fiddled around with a few other insignificant chores, then finally returned to the table. But she did not answer his question.

"This whole thing about you being worthy, about earning

your life. Is it because you feel guilty for living? I can understand that," he admitted. "I felt like that after Lisa died, as if I should've died in her place."

"No, I don't feel guilty. It's more like…" She gave up and shrugged. "It's hard to put into words."

"I'd like to understand what drives you," he said quietly. "I'd like to figure out what's behind this burning need you have to excel at everything. Even cooking." Kent waved a hand over the table. "I mean, look at what you've created here. You can hardly call this beginner's work. One dish, maybe that salad, or even the biscuits, that would have been a good start. But you've gone way beyond that and created this meal. Not that I'm complaining. It's fantastic and I've enjoyed it very much. But it's so—"

"Extreme?" Jaclyn made a face. "I never did do things by half measures, Kent, even in high school."

"No, you didn't." Kent was beginning to wish he could abandon the whole subject. It was none of his business and he felt like he was prying, but he desperately wanted to understand why she felt so driven. "Why is that?"

The kettle started to boil so she rose and made some hot tea which she carried to the table along with two mugs. She also laid out a platter of fruit, took away his empty plate and offered him a small bowl.

"You see," she said with a smile, "I didn't go whole hog and make dessert, too."

Kent remained silent and kept watching her. When he didn't speak she sighed. She set her elbows on the table then cupped her chin in her palms.

"It's like this. God spared me, so I need to make sure I don't waste a single moment. Like I have to make up for what Jessica didn't get to experience." Her voice was quiet, defensive. "Maybe that sounds stupid to you, but it's like a drive inside of me. I need to make sure I do everything as well as I possibly can, to earn what I've been given."

"But Jaclyn," Kent asked, his gaze never leaving her face. "When will you have earned it? When will you have done enough?"

"I don't know." Gravity filled her big brown eyes. Her lashes glittered with tears. "I just know that I can't fail. I can't mess up again." Jaclyn jumped up and strode across the room. She grabbed a tangle of vivid-colored threads and held it up. Her smile flashed. "Or my life will end up like this."

Kent rose from the table and walked slowly toward her. The threads were attached to a piece of white fabric held by some kind of stretcher bar. "Needlepoint?" he asked in confusion.

"Yes, needlepoint. I joined a stitchery class. I've been taking lessons from Heddy. She makes fantastic pictures and stuff. But I'm a dud at it." She shrugged as if it didn't matter, but he saw pain lurking in the depths of her expressive eyes.

"Does it matter, Jaclyn? You're good at so many other things. Does needlepoint really matter?"

"Yes!" She swiped away a tear. "Yes, it matters. A lot."

"Why? Because it will get you patients?"

"No. Maybe partly." She didn't look at him.

"But if you don't like it why subject yourself—" A sudden thought made him wince. "You're doing it because Jessica did it."

She nodded.

"But Jaclyn, you are not Jessica. You're you. You can't force yourself to be something other than yourself." His heart ached for this beautiful woman's lack of self-confidence. "You can't be more than who you are—a wonderful doctor. Do I think you need to get some patients? Yes. But not by becoming all things to all people. I really think you're shortchanging yourself by trying so hard to compensate for Jessica's death."

"It's not her death I'm trying to compensate for," she said, her voice filled with pathos. "It's her life." Then the tears did fall. Jaclyn stood there, looking so small and bereft that Kent couldn't help but wrap his arms around her.

"Oh, Jaclyn. Jessica doesn't need you to compensate for her life," he whispered, pressing her head against his shoulder. He threaded his fingers through her hair and pushed it back, away from her face. "Jessica lived her life and lived it well on her own terms. Don't you remember?"

"Not really. Sometimes I can hardly remember her at all." Jaclyn's forehead bumped his chin, her eyes full of despair.

"I can see her burying her nose in those daisies you used to bring her on Fridays, after you got paid. She adored them so much she wore them out just by touching them. I remember how you tried to coax her to learn how to ride bareback but she would have none of it." He closed his eyes and inhaled her soft sweet scent. "I remember she wouldn't even try certain vegetables they had in the cafeteria at school."

"Yes." Jaclyn laughed. "She was pretty stubborn about a lot of things."

"Yes, she was," he agreed. "You and I, and I'm guessing a lot of other people, remember those things about Jessica because they made her unique. As you are unique. So why do you think you have to live your life as if you are Jessica? You aren't, Jaclyn. You're you and you are the only person you owe anything to. That's what I meant about this morning's message."

She pulled away from him and frowned, which wrinkled her pert nose in the most adorable way. "What does this have to do with the sermon?"

Surprised by the loss he felt when Jaclyn stepped out of his arms, Kent scrambled to focus on what he'd been trying to get across to her. He followed her to the table, sat down and accepted the mug of tea she poured for him.

"Tell me what you mean," Jaclyn ordered.

"Well," he began, feeling his way, "David knew who he was. No matter how often he appealed to God to help him, he knew in his heart of hearts that he was God's, no matter what. He sinned, he made horrible mistakes, but he never lost sight of who he was as a child of God, or that God's love for him was unshakable."

Jaclyn studied him but said not one word. So he continued.

"That got me thinking," he continued, stuffing down his reluctance to discuss his personal life. If it would help Jaclyn, that was worth baring his soul. "I've always blamed myself for Lisa's death because I lit the fire that eventually killed her."

"But you didn't know she was there," Jaclyn protested.

"No, but I should have. I knew how depressed she was. I knew my refusing to leave the ranch would decimate her. She'd always held out hope that eventually I'd give up my plan to make Dad's dream come true, that I'd sell." He raked a hand through his hair, remembering that day too clearly. "The day she died I was tired, fed up with our bickering and the way nothing seemed to be going our way. I was also terrified that the wildfire would take everything we had. I felt like I had no control over anything and I lashed out at Lisa." He ignored the pressure of Jaclyn's fingers against his arm. He had to finish this. "Then I left to start the backfire. And she walked out into it."

"Oh, Kent." Jaclyn's eyes brimmed with tears as she met his gaze. Then something in her expression changed. Her eyes widened. "You think it was suicide. Don't you?"

"I don't know. That's what has hounded me all these years. Did I cause her to take her own life?" Kent rubbed the back of his neck to ease the tension there.

"I'm no expert on depression, but Brianna's told me about some cases she treated. Even if Lisa did choose suicide, it is not your fault." Jaclyn leaned toward him. "You cannot be held responsible for her decision."

"I feel responsible. There was a message on the phone. Maybe she came out to tell me, couldn't find me and when she was caught decided it was easier to give in than to fight. Maybe she didn't intend to get stranded. I just don't know." His voice was tortured.

"And you will never know." Jaclyn touched his cheek with her hand, her skin was soft against his. "That's the hardest part, not knowing. That's what you have to let go of."

"This morning made me realize that." He replayed the words of the sermon in his brain. "Lisa and I prayed for God's blessings on us and the ranch every single day. And still she died." It was like he was groping his way through a maze, trying to understand all he'd heard.

"So how does the sermon fit?" She leaned back, her face expectant.

"David was pursued by his enemies, injured and shamed for what seems like no reason. Yet each time he got up, faced his mistakes, rebuilt his faith in God and rebuilt his world." He glanced across the room, then smiled. "You know what, Jaclyn? I've been just like you with your needlepoint."

"You do needlepoint?" she teased, but empathy glowed in her dark gaze.

"Yeah, with cows." He chuckled at her puzzled face. "You hate needlepoint. You tangle the threads, make knots where there shouldn't be any and generally ruin the fabric. You keep pushing, even though that needlepoint is a mess and you're only making it worse."

"Well, thanks for that encouragement."

"I'm doing the same thing," Kent told her, amazed by his discovery. "I hate ranching but I keep on doing it, just like you keep doing that needlepoint, despite the fact that we both mess things up. I keep doing things my own stupid way despite my failures. I'd have lost the ranch and ruined everything Dad built if it wasn't for Dad's friend Gordon."

"Meaning?" Dubious about his point, Jaclyn tilted her head sideways as she waiting for him to complete his illustration.

"The point is I've been trying to force myself to do something I shouldn't be doing because I thought it would somehow make losing Lisa and my parents okay." Saying it lifted a heavy load from his heart. "The message today helped me see I can't change the past. Ranching isn't my forte."

"Ah." She sipped her tea. "Good. So you're going to build your sanctuary."

"I don't know. I'm not sure that's where I should be going, either." He finished his tea, carried his cup to the sink and rinsed it. "I need to get a handle on my life, to talk to God and to think things through. Right now I need to focus on finishing your clinic and getting the emergency plan for the town operational. Then I'll think about my future."

Kent stopped, debated the wisdom of saying the rest of what was in his heart. Jaclyn was an amazing woman dealing with a lot from her past, and maybe from her present, too, given her parents' objections to the clinic. He didn't want to add to her pain or confuse her, but neither did he want her get bogged down in guilt, as he'd been. He wanted, he realized, for her to be happy and content. He wanted the very best for her.

"Go ahead and say it, Kent." Jaclyn smiled. "I know you're itching to tell me something."

"You're doing the same thing as me. Trying to make something work that can't. You cannot earn your right to live, Jaclyn, and it doesn't matter how hard you try, you never will. Your life is a gift given to you by God because you're His child and He loves you dearly. You don't have to measure up. He already loves you."

Her face tightened with masked emotions. He forced himself to continue.

"You're wearing yourself out joining all these clubs, Jaclyn." Amazed by his own temerity but determined to make her take a second look at her life, Kent pressed on. "If the clinic is God's purpose for you, then maybe it's time for you to sit back, trust Him and let Him work out the details."

Jaclyn, her face flushed, opened her mouth to say something, but a piercing sound cut her off. Her eyes widened to huge brown orbs as she looked at him.

"Fire." Kent pulled out his keys. "I have to get to the station."

She was right behind him, closing the door and jogging to her car. "I need to get to the hospital in case there's something I can do."

He loved that she was so willing to jump into the fray and help however she could.

"Please think about what I said."

"Deal," she said. He squeezed her arm then climbed in his truck and drove away.

In the midst of a prayer for the safety of Hope's residents, Kent realized something else.

He'd broken all his own rules and fallen in love with Dr. Jaclyn LaForge.

Oh, God, you know that can't happen. You know I fail those I love. Please, take it away. I'd rather be alone for the rest of my life than hurt her.

But life without Jaclyn in it was a very bleak prospect.

Chapter Eleven

"You sound tired." Brianna Benson's voice transmitted concern across the phone line.

"I am," Jaclyn agreed. "There was a car accident outside of town today which caused a very bad fire." She rubbed her temples to ease the thudding there. "A coronary, burns, assorted bumps and bruises and a multitude of stitches were all a part of my day."

"Why you? You're not an emergency specialist," Brianna said.

"Here in Hope I am. This is a small town, remember? There aren't any specialists, per se. Lately I've been helping out on the emergency ward. This is the first time I've sat down since lunch." She smothered a yawn. "And then I stopped by the clinic."

"That sounds ominous." Brianna—a psychologist—had a gift for sensing trouble. "Want to talk about it?"

"Kent's not going to get it done in time." Jaclyn had known it subconsciously for days, but she'd kept hoping she was wrong. New water damage caused by a bad pipe had changed everything. Now there was no longer any point in pretending. "It won't be habitable by my deadline."

"Can you ask Kent to work harder?"

"No, I can't. He's already going all out." Bitter disappointment threatened to swamp her but Jaclyn pushed it back. "It's not Kent's fault. There's just too much for him to do and no one else to help." She sniffed. "I'm going to lose my funding, Brianna. The clinic isn't going to happen."

"I'm so sorry. Are you sure?"

"Pretty sure." Jaclyn told her a few of the many things that still needed to be done at the clinic.

"What about the townspeople? They used to be pretty gung ho on working together."

"That just shows you haven't been back in Hope for a while. This feud has split everyone. Nobody seems interested in helping anyone else. In fact, I still don't have many patients." Where did all this leave her, Jaclyn wondered? "Do you think I was wrong to start this?" she asked her friend.

"You've wanted to start that clinic for as long as I can remember," Brianna said. "There's nothing wrong with that."

"But maybe I've been going about it the wrong way." She reminded Brianna about all the groups she'd joined, all the ways she'd tried to become part of the small community. "I've tried to make them see I'm not the same kid that vandalized their church, but Kent was right. I'm killing myself trying to be all things to all people. Worse than that, it isn't working. Kent says—"

"Sounds like you and Kent have been talking a lot. Anything you want to tell me about him, Jaclyn?" The hint was hard to miss.

"I like him, Brianna. A lot." Understatement.

"You always did." A soft giggle. "Has he changed much from high school?"

"We all have. I suspect losing his parents and then his wife changed Kent most. He's been great, but friendship is all we can share. You know that."

"I don't know that at all." Brianna's voice softened. "I

only know you've told yourself that. All these years you've been so focused on getting Jessica's clinic on track that you haven't allowed anything else in your life. Maybe it's time to rethink that."

"Nothing's changed, Brianna," she said quietly. "Marriage isn't for me. I'm dedicated to my patients."

"To the exclusion of everyone and everything else? I don't think that's healthy. We all need people in our lives."

"That's the pot calling the kettle black. Who do you have?" Jaclyn challenged.

"My son. He fills my world with joy."

"Is that all you want?"

"For now it is," Brianna said. "He's got problems right now and I need to get his world straightened out. But if I'm being totally honest, I think I had my shot at love and blew it."

She was referring to dumping Zac right before their marriage. Jaclyn had never figured out exactly why Brianna had done that and her friend had always refused to discuss it.

"Zac's still here," she said. "Every so often he shows up to help Kent with the clinic. He's still single."

"Oh." Brianna was silent for a few moments. "So I should get involved but you won't consider it yourself?"

"I can't. It wouldn't be fair to the guy." She squeezed her eyes close and fought back the tears. "You know how my parents' marriage is, Brianna. Ever since Jessica died, they've been like strangers sharing a house. They loved each other once, but that's gone. I couldn't go through that—watching love die."

"There's no reason you have to. Not all marriages are like theirs. People can heal after a loss, if they're willing to work at it. Trust me, in my practice I've seen all kinds of rifts healed. But they have to do it in their own time and their own way. You're not responsible for them."

"But if they approved of my clinic—"

Kent knelt in front of her, took her bare foot in his hands and began to massage away the pain.

"You were a trouper today." His fingertips were so soothing she could barely keep her eyes open. "I realized something this afternoon, Jaclyn. That clinic of yours could be a huge asset in an emergency. We could use it as a triage center to handle minor injuries, people who are homeless, stuff like that. You've got some equipment that would be very useful."

"Uh-huh." Heart raging, she carefully lifted her foot out of his grasp. "Thank you. It's better now." She waited until he'd taken a seat opposite her. "But the clinic would have to be operational for that and I now realize that isn't going to happen."

"You're giving up?" He bent so he could peer into her eyes. "That easily?"

"Easily? It's not easy at all." She pushed back her hair and folded her legs beneath her, fighting the urge to give in to tears. "But it is reality and I'm not the kind of person who avoids the truth. The truth is you can't get the place operational in the two weeks we have left."

"Can't I?" His blue eyes glinted with an interior fire. "Actually that's why I'm here."

When Kent smiled his grin did odd things to her brain cells, muddling them. She wanted to put her foot back in his hands, just to have him touch her. Was this what love did to you?

"Are you listening to me?" he demanded. "You look—weird."

"Thank you. I feel weird." She nodded. "What's this idea?"

"Well, I know you originally wanted to call the place Jessica's Clinic, but after today, after seeing people in this town pull together to stop that fire the accident caused, I started thinking. Maybe they'd chip in and help finish the clinic if they felt they had some stake in it."

"You want me to offer shares?" She frowned at him in confusion. "That would take ages to arrange."

"No, doctor dearest." He brushed her nose with his fingertip. "I want you to sponsor a contest to name the clinic." He moved his fingers to cover her lips and stem her protest. "Just listen. You want the clinic open to honor your sister, right?" He waited for her nod. "But it's getting close to your deadline and opening might not happen. So how does it honor Jessica if the clinic doesn't open?"

She frowned again shifting so his hand fell away from her as she reconsidered.

"People saw you in action today, Doc, and they were impressed. They watched you pitch in unasked. They know you're good at what you do and I think they finally see that you're committed. Sooner or later I'm sure they'll come around, but we need them sooner."

"So?" She still wasn't sure how this could work.

He spread his hands wide and grinned, his whole face alive with excitement. "We make them feel like they have ownership in the clinic by appealing to them to help choose a name. That's inclusion and I think it will turn the tide. You've laid the groundwork, now it's time to see if joining all those committees paid off."

Jaclyn had let go of so many things. She'd had to relinquish the burnt-out building and make do with a smaller one. Brianna wasn't going to be able to join her as soon as she'd hoped because she couldn't sell her home in Chicago. Their friend Shay was supposed to come on board at the clinic in six months but now that arrangement was also in jeopardy. Now she had to relinquish Jessica's name?

"But if it isn't named for Jessica, how will people know about my sister?"

"If they don't know, will that lessen the impact? Will that

make Jessica's clinic any less valuable?" Kent leaned forward. "I know it's not the way you planned, Jaclyn. But it might be better. Can you take a chance on that?"

There it was again, the suggestion that she had to release control. Jaclyn squeezed her eyes closed. She could see her sister's face as if she were here now. She could hear the phrase she'd always repeated—let go and let God.

"Okay." She exhaled and opened her eyes.

"You'll do it?" Kent looked surprised.

Jaclyn nodded. "It's a good idea. How do we do it?"

"I brought some stuff to make signs. I say we hang them all over town." Kent opened the door, drew a big bag inside and began unloading markers and poster boards on her dining table. "We'll tell people to drop off their suggestions at the town hall. I've already talked to the staff there and it's okay with them."

"Pretty sure of yourself, weren't you?" She had to laugh at his confident grin.

"I know how much you want this clinic to happen." His gaze met hers. "I think this will ignite interest more than anything else we can do." He reached out and touched her shoulder then slid his palm up to cup her cheek. "We're not giving up on Jessica's clinic. No way, Doc."

We. She loved the sound of that. Like they were a team.

Overcome with emotion that this wonderful man had done so much for her, she leaned forward and brushed her lips against his cheek. "Thank you, Kent," she whispered, and meant it.

"You're welcome." Kent grinned. "So what are you waiting for? We've got work to do."

She sat down, pulled the cap off a black pen and began to print as the tall, dark and handsome rancher tossed his Stetson on her sofa and sat down beside her to get to work.

* * *

Kent arrived at the clinic at five the next morning with new resolve.

It had come yesterday, after he and his men had extinguished the fire caused by the rollover of a gasoline truck that had caused a three-car pileup. He'd gone to the hospital to have a minor burn treated and instead watched in amazement as Jaclyn dealt with the taxing of the little hospital's resources by assigning volunteers tasks without regard for the town feud. As a result, former enemies had cooperated in a common goal for the community and turned what might have been tragedy into triumph. Her actions had given him the idea for the contest. It had also inspired him to get the clinic finished.

Kent had spent a long time last night wishing he could build on the friendship he'd forged with Jaclyn. It would be so easy to love her.

But that wasn't going to happen.

Kent had failed Lisa—he knew and accepted that, and he was dealing with the guilt. But he could never trust himself to love Jaclyn, couldn't stand to let her down, to disappoint her. And disappointing people was what he did best. His parents, Lisa, even God. Yes, he was trying to change that, trying to be more trusting in God's love for him, but that didn't mean he was willing to risk hurting Jaclyn. So he ignored his feelings for her and got busy on her clinic.

At seven, Zac stopped by with a thermos of coffee and two doughnuts.

"Hey, cowboy, take a break." He looked around. "This place is coming together," he said with approval.

"Thanks, but we've got a long way to go yet." Kent paused, grateful for the snack since he'd managed only a meager breakfast.

"I can stop by after school and give you a hand," Zac offered. "I'm pretty good with a paintbrush. I could do the trim outside."

"Great! I've been meaning to touch that up. I wish I knew someone who was good with cement. The walkway is in terrible shape and I haven't got time to fiddle with it."

"I'll pray about it. Maybe God will send someone."

"Maybe He will," Kent said, trying to keep the faith.

No sooner had Zac left than someone else pounded on the door.

"Heddy promised us roast beef dinner with apple pie tonight if we helped you out today." Two former town council members stood there smiling. "Put us to work."

Knowing both men were dab handymen, Kent gave them the task of adding trim to the bathroom and examination rooms. He'd barely finished talking when two women arrived and offered to clean. More helpers trickled in throughout the day to repair the waiting-room chairs, to paint a mural, to hang shelves in each of the examining rooms. Each offer allowed Kent to place a tick beside another to-do item—even, finally, the much-needed cement work. God really was giving them a hand and Kent was thrilled.

Zac had just started painting the exterior trim when Joey's parents and three other couples appeared and insisted on tackling the ugly plot behind the building. Kent was dubious about their plans, but when he went to check on them, he found the area transformed into a parking stall for Jaclyn and a tiny walled-off garden bursting with flowers, the perfect place for staff breaks.

"This is lovely," he told them.

"It's the least we can do for Dr. Jaclyn," Joey's mom told him, her face glowing. "Because of her, our son will have an easier life. The specialist says he will walk without the pain after the operation."

So Jaclyn had been right about Joey's chances. Kent cringed as he remembered how he'd questioned her decision.

"If Dr. LaForge hadn't taken our daughter to that healing center in Las Cruces, she would never have entered drug treatment," another woman said. "This is our way of thanking her."

"We need Jaclyn in this town," said the third. "She makes us think about what Hope could be."

A rush of awe filled Kent. Jaclyn had given Hope so much. Now, finally, it was coming back to her. She was going to get the clinic she'd been dreaming of. He could hardly control his excitement. After everyone had left for the day, he did a walk-through and made a new list, much shorter and easier to complete. He'd received enough phone calls offering to help that the following day's tasks should be covered.

Thank You, God.

Part of him wanted to crow with pride at this amazing woman. Jaclyn's presence in Hope made a big difference to the town—and if he was honest, to him. He couldn't escape the truth—Jaclyn had dug herself a place in his heart.

But love? Love was too risky. The thought of failing Jaclyn, of seeing her beautiful face reflect her disappointment in him was untenable. Better not to go there. Better to remain friends…though he yearned to share so much more with her.

"Kent?" Jaclyn stood in the doorway, her confusion evident. "What happened?"

"Hope happened." He watched her smile flicker to life. "People have been stopping by all day to help. Two more days and, with a little push from heaven, the clinic should be ready to open. Early."

Without warning, she threw herself into his arms and hugged him so tightly he could barely breathe.

"Hey, are those tears?" he asked, drawing back to study her face. He wanted to pull her close, kiss her and promise her the world. But Kent contented himself with brushing the moisture off her cheeks. "This isn't the time for tears."

"No. You're right." She eased away and summoned a smile. "Can I see the rest?"

"Sure." He led the way, pointing out the changes.

"This is amazing. I can't thank you enough," she said when they arrived in the small garden.

"Don't thank me. I'm just the guy with the list. The people of Hope did the rest." He grinned, delighted with her happiness.

"Let's celebrate," she said. "I'll buy you dinner."

Watching those incredible eyes of hers sparkle made his heart thud ten times faster. He'd begun to imagine sharing a future with her, and it was dangerous territory. He had to escape before he got in any deeper. "I've got a couple of animals in quarantine. I need to get home."

"Oh. That's too bad." Did the light in her eyes dim just a bit? Good thing he was getting out of here now. Jaclyn La-Forge made him want things he couldn't have.

"Hello, you two. I hoped I'd still find you here. This looks lovely." Heddy took her time studying the work that had been done. "Just the place to enjoy the little dinner I brought." She held out a picnic basket.

"Heddy, I can't stay."

She ignored Kent's refusal and set out two plates, cutlery and a bunch of dishes that wafted enticing aromas when she lifted the lids.

"Oh, it smells wonderful," Jaclyn breathed. "Heddy, no matter how many cooking classes I take, I will never be able to make anything like this." She glanced at Kent. "You have to eat. Why not eat here?"

"Listen to the doctor," Heddy ordered.

"Okay, dinner," he agreed, shutting down the warning

voice in his head. "Then I have to get home." Kent allowed Heddy to serve him a plate. "It's very kind of you."

"We all want to help," Heddy said. "This is my way. That's the thing, isn't it? Figuring out how you can give. Lots of people in Hope wanted to give to you, Jaclyn. They just didn't know how."

"But—" Jaclyn showed her surprise.

"You joined all those groups, excelled at everything you tried—well, except for the needlepoint." She grinned. "Anyway, you've always pulled more than your share. Nobody believed you needed their help. It wasn't until the announcement about the contest that they started asking questions and learned the clinic might not open. That's when they found they could give to you."

Kent wondered if the blunt words hurt Jaclyn. She prided herself on giving and now Heddy was saying she needed to learn how to take.

"Actually, your clinic has been the best thing for this town. We needed something big to draw us together," Heddy explained. "Now, how about seconds?"

Kent said little as he savored the rest of Heddy's meal and the apple pie she'd brought for dessert. Jaclyn said even less, her eyes filled with wonder as she kept looking at her new clinic.

"I heard about this apple pie from two of my workers today." Kent blinked at the rush of rose that flooded Heddy's round cheeks.

"Oh, those two. They're neighbors on either side. A year after Henry died they both started asking me out. I'm not interested in romance," she sputtered.

"Why not?" Jaclyn touched her hand. "Just because you loved your husband is no reason you can't love again."

"I don't think I could feel what I felt for Henry for another man," Heddy murmured.

"Oh, Heddy, of course you couldn't." Jaclyn leaned forward, her voice quietly comforting. "Henry was special and your bond with him was forged over a long time. But maybe you could find a different kind of love."

"Oh, you'll make me cry now." Heddy patted her shoulder. "Love is strange, isn't it? It's hard to define but you know when you feel it."

"I think love is like elastic. It stretches and grows to allow our hearts to experience many different varieties, if we let it." Jaclyn turned her head and stared straight at Kent.

Discomfited by her penetrating stare, Kent glanced at Heddy and found she was peering at him. He ignored them both and hunkered down, concentrating on his pie.

"Kent, have you shown Jaclyn the glade yet?"

His head jerked up. He couldn't spend the evening with Jaclyn. She was already in his thoughts too much.

"Um, no." He gulped. "I haven't."

"Well, you're always talking about it. Wouldn't this be the perfect evening to show her?" Heddy took their plates. "Get going. Our spring evenings are longer now, but they don't last forever."

"Uh—" He could hardly decline now.

"Kent has some injured animals he has to check." Jaclyn rose and carefully replaced the dishes in the basket. "And I have some medical journals to study."

"You can look at them later," Heddy insisted as she nudged Jaclyn forward. "You deserve some time off, Jaclyn. The clinic will still be here tomorrow. Soon it'll be open and you'll be too busy."

"I'm not sure—" Though Jaclyn protested, Kent saw longing in her brown eyes and in that instant, his resolve evaporated.

"Why not?" he invited quietly. "The glade is really spectacular right now."

She blinked as if she didn't think she'd heard right. "You're sure?"

"I'm positive. Maybe you can bring Arvid back with you. I think his place here is about ready." He smiled at her while his heart thudded in anticipation.

Maybe he was taking a risk by inviting her out. For so long he'd stayed aloof from the possibility of any relationship. He hadn't wanted to be reminded of what he'd lost. But Jaclyn's arrival had shown him how desperately lonely he was—lonely for someone to share things with, lonely for conversation that wasn't just hello and goodbye.

But Kent wanted more than just company with Jaclyn. He wanted to know everything about her, to discover all the little details and file them away in his heart.

"Well, if you're sure I won't be imposing, I'd love to go," she said. "Your glade sounds like the perfect place to restore my sanity."

"Can you be at the ranch in half an hour?" he asked.

"Yes. For once I'm not on call." Jaclyn's gorgeous smile made his heart race.

Kent turned to Heddy and hugged her.

"You're a manipulator, Heddy Grange," he whispered in her ear. "And I shouldn't let you do it. But because you're such a fantastic cook, I'll fall in with your plans. Thank you for everything," he added meaningfully, glancing around. "I know you were behind it."

"No, Kent. Thank you. God has special blessings reserved for those who put themselves out there for others. Hope's going to be fine," she said quietly. "Are you?"

Before he could answer she'd bustled away, toting her empty basket.

"I'd better go. See you in a bit?" he said

Jaclyn smiled at him and headed out to her car.

Maintaining nothing but friendship between them wasn't

going to be easy. Now that he knew he was in love with her, he'd weakened enough to imagine a future that included sharing the ranch, marriage, maybe even a family.

"Don't be ridiculous," he scolded himself. "She's a doctor, a busy doctor. Why would she want to live on a ranch miles outside of town?"

Maybe if he showed her the beauty of the ranch—

"Stop it." Kent recognized his daydreams for what they were—hope. Hope that he could finally be done with the guilt, the shame, the failure, and find peace.

Heddy said God had special blessings reserved for him, but given his record of failure, Kent was pretty sure those blessings weren't going to involve Jaclyn LaForge.

"What if I fail again?" he said as he pulled into his yard. "I'd mess up her future here."

So what do I do, God?

But if God had some wisdom about Kent's future, He wasn't sharing it.

Chapter Twelve

"I can't talk right now, Shay. I'm on my way out to Kent McCloy's ranch for a horse ride." Jaclyn fumbled the phone and so only caught the tail end of her friend's next words.

"...talked to Brianna." Shay sounded hesitant. "Is something going on with you and Kent?"

"Nothing's going on. We're just friends." She found her sweater hanging on a kitchen chair.

"Oh." Shay sounded totally different from the strong, powerful image of her gracing magazine covers around the world. "Brianna said you have feelings for Kent?"

"I do." With a huff of resignation, Jaclyn sat down. "I love him. He makes me feel that I don't have to prove anything, that I'm all right."

"Aren't you all right?" Shay's timid voice strengthened. "Brianna is right, Jaclyn. It's not your job to fix the whole world. I never thought God expected you to make amends for Jessica's death or your parents' marital problems." She paused then asked very quietly, "Do you?"

"No," Jaclyn admitted. "I'm realizing that to honor Jessica, I have to stop trying to live her life. But something happened that has proven to me that I'm on the right track here." She told her friend how she'd given up on getting the clinic finished before her deadline, and about how the town showed up en masse to make opening possible. "It's amazing how much they've done and all because of a little contest."

"So have you chosen a new name?"

"Not yet." Jaclyn eyed the shopping bag full of suggestions that sat by the front door. "I guess I could choose one this evening, with Kent. After all, the contest was his idea."

"When is the grand opening? Will your parents come?" Shay asked.

"No. They feel I made a mistake coming here and that given enough time, I'll change my mind." She squeezed her eyes closed to stop the tears. "I'm worried about divorce, Shay. They haven't said anything but I can tell there's something off."

"Jaclyn, I think fixing their marriage is up to them. You can't do it for them," Shay murmured.

"I know. I'm learning that God has specific things for me to do and that I have to let go of some things if I'm going accomplish His will. I still believe He wants me here in Hope, ministering to children."

"I think the clinic's completion by the townsfolk is proof of that," Shay agreed.

"But I don't know what to do about Kent," she murmured. "I don't want to end up in a relationship like my parents and Kent is so stuck on the past and all the things he did wrong."

"I'm not an authority." Shay said. "But perhaps if you told him how you feel, he'd realize that there can be a fulfilling future for him."

"Tell him I love him? Oh, I don't know, Shay." Her insides quivered at the thought.

"Isn't it better to see how he feels about it up front. Be honest." Shay paused. "If it was me, I guess I'd tell him, then accept his answer. At least then there won't be any confusion about it."

"I'll think about it." Jaclyn checked her watch. "Much as I love talking to you, I have to go. Call me tomorrow?"

"Okay. And Jaclyn? I hope Kent realizes what you're of-fering him. You deserve the best." A little catch in her voice stopped Shay.

"So do you, Shay. So do you. Don't forget, when it's fin-ished, the clinic will be waiting for you. I need you here."

Shay hesitated before she finally said, "I'll try to come as soon as I can. I promise. Bye."

Jaclyn hung up, grabbed the bag of contest entries and raced out the door. She made it to the ranch in just over forty-five minutes.

"Sorry," she apologized when she found Kent with the horses, waiting at the corral. "Shay called just as I was leav-ing."

"Is she coming to join the clinic?" He helped her mount.

"Not right away." A pang of guilt assailed her—all they'd talked about were her problems. "Is this glade of yours far, Kent?"

"Fifteen minutes." He frowned at the bag she'd looped over the saddle horn. "What's in there?"

"The contest entries. I thought maybe we could choose a name tonight."

"Have you read them over yet?" he asked, grinning at her.

"No. I thought we could do that together." She smiled back as she thought about what Shay had suggested. Could she do it? Could she just tell Kent how she felt and leave the rest to God?

They followed a switchback trail halfway up a hill then turned off into a grove of cottonwoods. The bright green of the freshly budded leaves whispered a welcome as they passed under. Jaclyn had to concentrate on negotiating the treacher-ous stony path and didn't understand why Kent had stopped until she looked up.

"It's an oasis," she gasped. "Kent, it is so beautiful here. I can understand why you want to stay on the ranch. This place is too precious to give up." She dismounted and wandered under a weeping birch tree to the edge of pretty little brook that bubbled through the glade. She sat on a rock, removed her boots and let her toes dangle in the cool water. "Fantastic."

Jaclyn turned and caught him staring at her. As soon as their eyes met, he looked away. Maybe he did feel something.

"I built a bench," he said when a few moments had passed. She followed his gaze to a crudely made bench—a combination of old logs hammered together into a seat and back. He sat down on it. "I come here a lot. To think."

"It's the perfect place," she agreed, keeping her voice quiet—the clearing seemed to call for reverence. "I suppose we should go over the contest entries before it gets too dark to see." She padded over the lush growth barefoot, carrying her boots. "Would you mind getting the sack from my saddle?"

He'd fastened the horses' reins under a shady cottonwood tree. "All of these?" he asked, as he lifted the sac.

She nodded.

"Wow. I never imagined so many people would enter."

"Me, neither. What it means is that we have a lot to go through." She lifted out a stack of entries. "Why don't we each take half, choose our favorites, switch piles and then compare? I brought a couple of pencils to mark which we like best." She glanced up and found his eyes fixed on her face but she couldn't read them. "Okay?" she asked when he didn't answer.

"Sure." He accepted half and began reading. Jaclyn couldn't help noticing he marked a lot of the sheets.

"We're supposed to be eliminating," she reminded with a grin.

"I know. But some of these are so catchy. Clinic of Cures," he read. "How can you not like that?"

"Trust me, it's not that difficult." She laughed.

They worked together in silence and then traded. Jaclyn waited with impatience for Kent to finish the last half dozen. When he finally raised his head and peered at her through the growing dusk, there was a peculiar light in his eye.

"You have a favorite?" he asked. She nodded. He smiled. "I think I know which one. It's Whispering Hope Clinic, isn't it?"

"Yes." She gathered the rest of the papers and pushed them back into the bag. "We sang that song in youth group, remember? According to the entry, Septimus Winner wrote the lyrics to 'Whispering Hope' in 1868. But those words embody everything I want for Jessica's clinic today." She wondered if Kent was as moved as she. Jaclyn began to sing the words to the song. "'Soft as the voice of an angel, breathing a lesson unheard. Hope with a gentle persuasion, whispers her comforting word.'"

Kent's voice joined her.

"'Wait till the darkness is over, wait till the tempest is done, hope for the sunshine tomorrow, after the shower is gone.'"

She smiled at him as they raised their voices together for the chorus.

"'Whispering hope, oh, how welcome thy voice, making my heart in its sorrow rejoice.'"

The notes died away. Silence filled the lovely glade broken only by the whisper of the cottonwood leaves.

"Whispering Hope Clinic," Jaclyn murmured. "It's the perfect name. Heddy was bang on. She's the winner."

"Yes." Kent smiled, blue eyes aglow. He shook his head. "I don't know what changed, but that woman is not the same one I've been battling with for the past few years."

"People do change, Kent. I've changed." Jaclyn knew it was now or never—this was her chance to tell him what lay in her heart. She was going to do it. "I came to Hope determined to work my way to acceptance. I thought I had to fix things and people. I thought I had to sacrifice myself to deserve life." She held his gaze. "A lot of people, including you, have helped me see how wrong I've been. I look at the clinic and the way the whole town has pitched in and I realize that sometimes people need to give and that the best thing I can do for them is to accept. Believe me," she said with a grimace, "it's humbling to realize that if I just get out of the way, God is fully able to heal. I've found it hard to learn that I am simply a tool He uses. I'm not the big deal I thought I was."

"I think you're a very big deal, Jaclyn." His solemn face told her he was serious.

"It was you and your questions about me earning my right to live that started me asking questions of myself. Because of you, I'm learning what it means to be a child of God, free of expectations from others and myself."

"That's good."

"Yes, because it opened my eyes to something else." Jaclyn took a deep breath. "I finally accepted that I'm in love with you. I have been for a while."

"Jaclyn, I can't—"

"No," she begged, placing her hand across his lips. "Let me finish. Please?"

He finally nodded.

"I know you've suffered. I know you don't think you deserve love, just as I thought I didn't deserve life unless I could earn it." She moved her hand, her eyes filling with tears as she stared at his beloved face. "That's a lie that we've both believed for too long."

"Is it?" His voice was barely a whisper.

"Yes, it is. You are a wonderful man, Kent. You devoted yourself to your wife, to this ranch, to your father's dream without regard for yourself. You devoted your time to making Hope a better place to live."

"I'm no hero."

"But you are. You're the only hero I've ever known." She swallowed hard. "You're full of love and you share it. Who else would have put up with Heddy for so long? Who else would bother to organize an emergency measures plan and make sure the whole town was included?"

Kent's expression gave nothing away. Jaclyn forced herself to go on.

"Those are just a few things I love about you. Maybe you think you're incapable of love, but I see you giving love every day—in the clinic, as mayor, as a friend. Whenever I think about my future, you're in it, Kent, and no matter how I try to pry out that love for you, it won't go. I love you."

"You can't." His blue eyes blazed.

She had to smile at the vehemence in those words. "But I do."

"Then you'll have to get over it because I can't love you, Jaclyn. I won't." His tanned face hardened so it looked like a mask. "And you know why."

She rose and stood in front of him, mere inches away, determined to force him to explain. "What is it about me you can't love?" *God, please give me courage.*

For a moment his hands rested on her shoulders and she thought he would kiss her. Then he shook his head, backing away when she stepped closer. "I think you're fantastic. If I could be in a relationship with anybody, Jaclyn, it would be you. But I can't."

"Maybe you only think you can't," she answered, her heart sinking like a stone.

"No. I know I can't." He looked over her shoulder, his stare intent, as if he could see the past. "I loved my wife. I loved her more than anything. But I couldn't help her. I couldn't protect her. She died because of me."

"Lisa died because she ran into a fire. You couldn't have known she was going to do it."

"I should have known. I was her husband—that was my job."

"To stop her from doing what she wanted?" Jaclyn shook her head. "Your 'job' was to love her, Kent. And you did. Cherish *those* memories, not the horrible ones you've been dredging up over and over."

She watched a host of emotions flicker across his face. His eyes narrowed and darkened; his jaw tightened.

"Lisa's not the only one I failed," he murmured.

"Kent you have to know your parents never thought you failed them."

"I'm not talking about my parents." Kent held her gaze, his hands clenched at his sides.

Kent stood, grasped the reins of the horses and handed her one set. He waited as she mounted Tangay, handed her the bag of contest entries and then climbed up on his own horse. His face looked like carved stone.

"Lisa was my last mistake, Jaclyn. It doesn't matter how much I might care about you, I will never again put myself in a personal relationship where I can fail someone I care about. I couldn't stand to watch you trying to cope when I let you down."

"But Kent, Lisa was sick."

"And I made it worse. I chose this land over my wife. What kind of a man does that make me?"

She didn't know what to say as she followed him from the sweet peaceful glade back to the ranch. Once there he took Tangay's reins and told her in cold, hard tones that he had to take care of the animals.

Kent's good-night sounded like a death knell. On the drive home, Jaclyn could only pray that somehow God would heal him. When she got to her place, she phoned Brianna to tell her what had happened.

"What will you do now?" her friend asked.

"Maybe I'll—" She stopped and corrected her train of thought. "That's my old way of thinking, that I could earn his love."

"I think the question is, Jaclyn, is Kent what you want? More importantly, do you think he's what God has planned for your future?" Brianna said.

"Yes, to both. I believe Kent is the man God has chosen for me." The truth of those words sank in.

"So now you proceed to live your best life, walking in faith, being honest with Kent and depending on God's love."

"Exactly." The advice was bang on. "Thanks, Brianna. Sorry I called so late." She hung up with new resolution.

Jaclyn opened her Bible and reread the sections she'd underlined, pressing the promises into her heart and soul. Then she prayed for God to lead her.

"It's not over, Kent McCloy," Jaclyn said fiercely. "Maybe you've given up, but I will not let go of you that easily."

Chapter Thirteen

Through sheer grit and determination Kent finished Whispering Hope Clinic the following day. He attended the grand opening two days later and even managed to give a short speech, but when the event turned into a block party, he left as quickly as he could, pretending he didn't see Jaclyn watching him, and that he hadn't been watching her.

But back at the ranch he found it difficult to concentrate. He did little but sit and daydream as his mind replayed Jaclyn's words of love over and over.

Two days after his rush to get out of Hope, he was back in town, sitting with the old coots on coffee row and hoping to hear something, anything, about Jaclyn. He missed her big smile, her infectious chuckle and the way she always brought him food, as if she thought he was starving.

He missed her voice. He missed talking to her. He missed her.

"What are you doing mooning around here?" Chester Crumb demanded when Kent arrived at his coffee shop Crumb Cakes for the third morning in a row. "Thought you were building some kind of animal refuge or something."

"Who told you that?" But Kent already knew.

"Doc mentioned last night that you had a hankering to do

something like that. Keeps awful hours, she does." Without being asked Chester served him a piece of steaming apple pie. "You got that done already?"

"Uh, no. I came to town for supplies," Kent said, knowing he'd now have to go to the building store and get some timber and plywood.

Back at the ranch he changed into his work clothes, faced himself in the mirror and got a grip. First, he needed to focus on clearing up all the things he should have handled long ago. One of those things was the cattle. He picked up his radio and asked his hired hand to come to the house.

"So that's my price for the cattle," he said to a stupefied Gordon. "You more than anyone understand Dad's dream. I hope you're successful."

"All of them?" Gordon frowned at his nod. "You're sure about this?"

"Positive. I failed to make his dream come true but I believe you will." Kent held out his hand to shake on the deal. "Best of luck," he said.

"But what are you going to do with the ranch?" Gordon asked.

"I'm not sure yet."

But he *was* sure. Kent knew exactly what he was going to do. He'd agonized over it too long. It was time to sell. Only before he did, he was going to build some small rescue shelters for the local wildlife department, something better than their current lean-tos. It would keep him from thinking about the future too much. Since he had the material, he set to work immediately.

By the time the supper hour rolled around and Zac stopped by, Kent had made a good start. He invited his friend to stay for a steak dinner.

"Did you say you're selling the ranch?" Zac frowned at the steak Kent had cooked him. "Are you nuts?"

"Maybe I am." Kent appreciated his friend's concern. "But it's time. I listed it today. There are too many memories here. I need to break free," he said.

Zac probably thought he meant Lisa, but in fact, Kent kept seeing Jaclyn—in the kitchen with those ridiculous red towels, chasing after kids at the birthday party, telling him she loved him in the glade. That last one had hounded him through several sleepless nights.

From what he'd heard in town, Jaclyn's clinic was going great. She belonged in Hope. But he didn't. He couldn't avoid her forever and it was getting too painful to see her beautiful face and not pull her into his arms and pretend everything would work out, that he wouldn't mess up again. So he'd move.

"If you're leaving, why bother building stuff?" Zac asked.

"They're a gift," Kent told him. "And I'm building them because they need them. I've talked about it for so long, it's time to put my money where my mouth is."

"What about Jaclyn?" Zac's voice was low and filled with concern.

"I predict a great future for her." Kent had replayed Jaclyn's confession of love over and over in his head, amazed that she'd had the strength to confront him with her feelings and loving her for it. Unfortunately he couldn't do anything about it. That way lay disaster.

"But she's in love with you. Any fool can see that. Didn't she tell you?"

"Yes, she did. It might have been easier if she'd never said those words," Kent told him. "But I'm sure she'll forget them before too long."

"That's not worthy of you or Jaclyn, cowboy. She's not hankering after chocolate. She *loves* you." Zac shoved back his chair and studied him. "What's wrong with you? Where are all those dreams you used to spout?"

"They're gone. I'm finished with dreams. I'm digging into reality now and reality means moving on." Kent pushed away his plate. Not even his favorite food grilled to perfection could ease the ache in his soul. He knew he would never get over Jaclyn LaForge. He rose and carried his plate inside. He had to do something or explode.

"Did you ever get around to reading those Psalms the pastor talked about?" Zac followed him into the house, carting some dishes with him.

"Uh, no, I guess I didn't. I've been meaning to but with the clinic—" He let the excuses trail away knowing his friend saw through them.

"I did. They were quite an eye opener. Maybe you should read them, too."

Once the meal was cleaned up, Zac excused himself and left, saying that with the end of the school year approaching he was buried with work.

Kent sat in the courtyard listening to the hum of the cicadas.

No matter how I try to pry out that love for you, it won't go. I love you. Jaclyn's words.

No, he was not going to go there again.

Kent took Oreo for a walk, but remembered Jaclyn ruffling the dog's fur. He checked on his chickens and two wolf cubs the wildlife guys had brought him, but that reminded him of the time he and Jaclyn had seen the wolf. He even washed the dishes and dried them on her red towels. Her words would not be silenced.

I love you.

Finally he threw the towel on the counter.

"Please make this go away because I can't do it, God. I will not take the risk of failing her."

Unable to even consider sleeping, Kent returned to the courtyard. Mindful of Zac's words, he took out his Bible and began to read the Psalms from beginning to end. Sometime later the flash of car lights swinging into his yard broke into his meditations. Jaclyn burst out of her car and stomped toward him.

"You're selling the ranch and leaving Hope." It was not a question.

"Yes."

"Because of me. Because I said I love you." She clapped her hands on her hips and dared him to refute it.

"Partly. But mostly because of me." He wanted to hug her, to erase the dark circles under her beautiful eyes. "I need to move on."

"Really. This need hit you all of a sudden, huh?" Her glance was scathing. "Just tell me one thing, Kent. And answer honestly." She waited until he finally nodded. "Do you love me?"

He gulped. She deserved the truth. It would be the last time they'd talk—he'd make sure of that. He'd attend another church until he sold the ranch. He'd already resigned as mayor. He'd get his groceries elsewhere, anything to keep from hurting her further.

"It's really not that difficult to answer, Kent. Do—you—love—me?" The moon backlit her figure in a hazy glow.

"I'm sorry, Jaclyn, but I can't be what you want me to be." He steadied his voice and continued with resolute determination. "I might love you now but—"

"So you do love me." Her face crumpled. "Then why won't you take a chance on us?"

"I can't. I wouldn't be good for you, Jaclyn."

"And the fact that I love you, that doesn't make a difference?"

He shook his head. Pain raced across her face but he couldn't let it sway him. He had to protect her. "I can't be trusted."

Jaclyn stared at him for a long time. Tears dripped down her cheeks and fell onto the white silk shell she wore. Finally she lifted her head and marched over to stand in front of him, eyes blazing.

"You're right, Kent. You can't be trusted. You can't be trusted because you won't be honest, not with me and not with yourself." She dashed away the tears with the back of her hand then reached out and poked him in the chest. "You're running scared. You've hidden out for so long, afraid to really live, afraid to take a chance because something bad might happen. You're willing to sacrifice our happiness because you're an emotional coward who won't take a risk."

She was furiously, blazingly angry. And he loved her.

"Well, guess what? Something bad will happen. Life isn't a sure thing. The Bible says 'Rain falls on the good man and the evil man,'" she quoted. "How dare you tell me or anyone else in Hope to go after our dreams when you refuse to dream at all? Everyone in town looks up to you, but you're an imposter, Kent. You talk big but you're afraid to put your money where your mouth is."

"I guess you're right." He wasn't going to argue. He could take her anger but he would never survive the pain when he failed her.

Jaclyn shook her head at him. "The only sure thing about life is, there is no sure thing. Living is risky, but what's the alternative?"

He had a hunch she had a lot more to say, but she was cut off by her beeper. Then his cell phone rang.

"I have to go," she said when he closed his phone. "I'm needed at the hospital."

"A fire," he told her as fear snaked down his spine and took up residence in his knees. "Some kids playing with matches started a fire in some brush. It's out of control and heading for the hospital. They've activated the emergency response system."

"I told you," she whispered, staring at him. "Bad comes to everyone. No one is exempt. What matters is how you handle it." She leaned forward and touched her lips to his. "Good-bye, Kent. I love you."

It took every ounce of willpower he possessed not to say the same thing to her. But what good would that do? So he climbed in his truck and followed her car down the hill, both of them exceeding the speed limit as, in the distance, the orange-gold haze of flames lit up the desert night sky.

As he drove, Kent prayed that God would keep her safe.

"They've sent word, Dr. LaForge. We have to evacuate. They can't hold the fire back any longer. We have to move." The nurse stared at her, fear threading through her words.

"Well, we expected that, didn't we?" Jaclyn said calmly. "We always take precautions where our patients are concerned. Do you have the procedure sheet?"

The nurse held it out. Jaclyn took it and began directing the removal of patients from the small hospital. Somewhere out there she knew Kent and his men were making every effort they could to put out the flames before they reached the hospital. All she could do was beg God to protect the man she loved and continue doing her job.

Sometime during the removal of the surgical patients, Heddy arrived.

"I thought you were at central control," Jaclyn said.

"Everything is in order there. They don't need me. Do you?" She looked scared and very pale.

"Indeed I do." Jaclyn paused a moment to hug her. "I need someone capable to keep the children calm while we get them out. Can you do that?"

"If I can't, I'm not much use on this committee, am I?" the older woman sputtered.

"I don't think I've ever told you what a blessing you are to this town, Heddy. Thank you." Jaclyn gave her another hug. "Go with Nurse Becky, will you?"

Heddy hurried away looking less stressed. Jaclyn answered her cell phone.

"Mom, hi. I can't talk now. I'm in the hospital in the middle of an emergency evacuation. A fire is threatening the town."

"What!" Her mother screeched for her husband then asked a flood of questions.

"Mom, I don't have time. Really. I've got to get the kids out of here. I'll call you later. I love you both."

"We love you, too, honey." The phone went silent.

Jaclyn stood where she was, stunned by those words. Her mother loved her. Tears rushed to her eyes and she dashed them away. How long she'd waited to hear those words. Years. Since Jessica's death. She'd tried so hard, done everything she could, but her mother had never actually said those words until today.

"Thank You, Lord," she whispered.

She nodded to the two nurses waiting for instructions. "Okay, let's get the three kids in wheelchairs out first. Sandra, you, Becky and Heddy take them. Once you're safely across, watch for me. I'll walk out the ambulatory ones. Ready?" She smiled at them. "Let's do this."

All they had to do was cross the street to the pool at the community center. The up-to-date fire suppression system there would protect her patients until the fire was out.

"Heddy, you follow Becky. Sandra, you're in the rear. Don't run, but keep moving. Apparently the smoke is fairly heavy outside so I want you both to wear the masks and make sure the kids have them on, too." She followed them to the exit doors and waited until they were ready, then nodded. "Go."

Heddy pushed the wheelchair across the street, battling the wind, the clouds of smoke and the uneven terrain. Every so often she paused to help Becky and Sandra with their chairs. Finally they stood in front of the doors of the complex. They turned to wave. Jaclyn was next. She took a moment to look around outside but although the fire seemed much closer now and she saw firemen racing to and fro, she could not spot Kent.

Please keep him safe.

Heddy's frantic waved signaled Jaclyn to go.

Just as Jaclyn finished explaining what would happen to the two little girls, someone handed her a child to carry. She ordered the other two to hang on to her and they began the crossing. But as she stepped off the sidewalk, a truck bearing a load of oxygen tanks burst onto the street and roared toward them, desperate to escape the licking tongues of flame eating up bushes in the compound where the tanks were kept.

Jaclyn waited for the truck to pass, silently begging the driver to hurry. In the same moment, she heard a snap. The straps holding the load of oxygen canisters broke, releasing everything. One tank flew over her head and hit the curb near a shrub now smoldering from the creeping fire.

"Run!" someone yelled.

Jaclyn ran, dragging the children with her. She was almost across when an explosion shook the ground beneath her feet. Debris flew through the air, smashed into parked cars and covered the ground around her. It was too risky to keep going—she shoved the children down and then covered them with her body.

Something stung as it grazed her hand, but it was the crack against her skull that made Jaclyn woozy. When she reached to touch her aching head, pain flared in a wave so strong she yelped. The world wobbled and stars flew. Beneath her the kids whimpered.

"Lie still, Jaclyn. Lie very still. I'm here. I'll look after you." Kent was there easing the children from under her and handing them to someone nearby. "Hang on, Doc. I'm going to take care of you."

"Kent?" Excruciating pain radiated through her head but she had to speak, she had to tell him.

"Yes?" He leaned near, his face an inch from hers so he could hear her wheezing words.

"I love you."

There was more, so much more she wanted to say but spears of silver light darted through her eyes. The agony enveloped her and everything went black.

Chapter Fourteen

If he lived to be ninety, Kent didn't think he'd ever forget the terror that gripped him when he saw the blood seeping from Jaclyn's head. In a daze he screamed for help. Moments later an ambulance attendant pushed him out of the way and bent over her. After a quick check, he twisted his head to look at Kent.

"Get that fire out," he said, his face grave. "We need that hospital."

Kent took one last look at Jaclyn's pale face, pressed a kiss to her hand then went back to work, pushing himself even harder. More afraid than he'd ever been, he kept a steady stream of prayers for Jaclyn going heavenward as he battled the raging inferno. Nobody had to tell him her injury was serious—he knew it. In the depths of his heart he knew he might never see her again and it was killing him.

Why didn't I tell her I loved her? Why didn't I, for once, take the risk? Because she's right. I am a coward.

All night he fought until finally the fire was extinguished and the hospital was safe. Only then did he give in to his desperation to know Jaclyn's condition.

"How's Jaclyn?" he asked over and over, but no one seemed to know where or how she was. Finally he found Heddy.

"Where is she?" he demanded. "Why isn't anyone telling me anything?"

"They air-lifted her to Las Cruces. We just heard that her head injury is very serious." Heddy's somber expression scared him. "One of the EMTs told me the hospital called her parents."

Kent had to see her. He turned to head for his truck, but stumbled from sheer weariness. Someone gripped his arm.

"Come on, Kent. You need to rest," Zac said. "You can pray for Jaclyn at home."

But Kent wasn't going home.

"I have to see her," he said and yanked his arm free. "I need to see Jaclyn."

Heddy exchanged a glance with Zac then nodded.

"I'll drive you." Zac pulled out his keys.

"Wait a minute." Kent shrugged out of his suit, walked over to one of his men and handed it to him. "You're in charge, Pete. I have to leave. Be careful."

"You know it. You tell Jaclyn we're praying for her." The other man slapped his shoulder.

"Kent?" Heddy had never looked more unkempt, but her heart was in her eyes as she said, "I'm praying for you both."

Kent got in Zac's car for the long drive to Las Cruces, wondering what he would say to Jaclyn when he got there. Because the fear he'd carried for so long was now bigger and stronger than ever. He loved her. Kent admitted that. But when had love ever been enough?

"Don't let her die," he begged God. "Please don't let her die."

When Kent made no headway with the medical staff at the Las Cruces hospital, Zac pushed him aside and told the nurse in charge that Kent was Jaclyn's fiancé. Finally someone agreed Kent could sit with her, but only Kent.

"Don't wait for me," he told Zac but his friend shook his head.

"I'm not going anywhere, cowboy. I'm going to sit here and pray."

"Thanks, pal." Kent followed the nurse down the hall. The surgeon met him.

"She's not fighting," the doctor told him. "Medically we've done all we can. Now it's up to her. If you can think of anything, say anything you think would help, do it. This is the time to pull out all the stops."

Kent watched him go, fear clutching at his throat as he pushed open the door and walked inside.

Jaclyn's room was small with a large window that let in the moonlight. She lay on the bed, pale and lifeless except for the machine that beeped at her side. A rock formed inside him. She gave love so easily. Jaclyn deserved to be loved back. She deserved someone who could appreciate her and return her love. She should be happy.

She still could be.

Kent pushed that thought away. His latest actions proved he couldn't give her what she needed, but he wanted her to be happy.

But when he studied the curve of her cheek, the silvery blond hair framing her face, the rock in his chest grew.

You're willing to sacrifice our happiness because you're an emotional coward who won't take a risk.

He picked up Jaclyn's hand, threading his fingers between hers. The rock grew heavier.

You're always running scared, Kent. You've hidden out for so long, afraid to really live, afraid to find a new dream, afraid to take a chance because something bad might happen.

She was right. He was an emotional coward because he told himself he was trying to protect her when really he was afraid to be vulnerable. He'd always been the strong one, the one his parents and his wife had depended on. But Kent wasn't strong.

And he was sick of pretending he was.

At this moment he was more scared than he'd ever been.

But as he studied her lovely face, he realized that he'd do anything to ensure Jaclyn's happiness, suffer anything to see her smile and laugh again.

He gulped. He'd do anything. Take a chance? But what if—

The Lord is my light and my salvation; Whom shall I fear? The Lord is the defense of my life; Whom shall I dread? The verses of the twenty-seventh Psalm played through his head, pushing light into the crevices and revealing the real cause of his fears.

Me. I'm the reason I'm scared. That's why he'd wasted so many years. That's why he hadn't been able to believe that God understood his situation—because he'd put his faith in himself instead of in God. But God wasn't limited by Kent McCloy's fears. God had a bigger picture. And because God was love, He forgave the past and gave new dreams for the future—a future with Him at the center.

Jaclyn was right. There would be problems in the future, some of them serious if her injury—no. He wouldn't think like that.

Be strong and let your heart take courage. Wait for the Lord.

"Okay, Lord," he prayed out loud. "I'm scared, I've messed up everything. Instead of depending on you to make a difference in Hope, I've been depending on myself to stop bad things from happening. I've been afraid of failing, as I have so often. But that changes right now. I accept Your love for me. I accept Your forgiveness. And most of all, I accept Your will for my life, whatever happens. It's in Your hands. Now, please take my fear and help me move into the future You have waiting for me."

He gazed at the small figure lying motionless under the white sheets.

"It's up to you, God. I'll trust you."

The rush of sweet forgiveness, the warmth of love everlasting filled his heart and chased out the fear that had resided there for so long. He stared into the face of the woman he loved and knew what he had to say. He bent and whispered in Jaclyn's ear.

"I have big dreams, sweetheart. But they can only come true if you're there to help me." Courage grew until the rock inside him crumbled and melted away. "I need you, Jaclyn. I love you. Please, don't give up on me because I'm not giving up on you. I'm here for however long you need me."

Jaclyn had been in a coma for nearly three weeks, and Kent was losing faith. So each day, before Kent drove to the hospital, he rode out to the glade to find a wildflower he could take to her. The glade had always been his special place and it was here he felt closest to God.

Kent spent an hour by the bubbling brook, just talking to his Savior as he sought to renew his waning courage. On the way out of the glade, he cut some daisylike chocolate flowers that were nestled in between some rocks. He dampened his handkerchief and wrapped it around the stems to preserve the delicate blooms for her. Then he rode back home, got in his car and drove to Las Cruces.

When he arrived at the hospital he found the hall outside Jaclyn's room teeming with people.

"What's going on?" he demanded then pushed into her room. Her parents stood by Jaclyn's bedside, hand in hand.

"Hi," he said, confused by their big smiles. They stood in front of the bed blocking his view. "What's up?"

"Me, actually." Jaclyn peeked around her mother.

Kent dropped his bouquet and stared at his beloved doctor.

"She woke up this morning and asked for breakfast," her mother said. "They'll do some tests later, but she seems fine."

"I am fine." Jaclyn stared straight at him. "Just a little confused. Apparently I acquired a fiancé while I've been asleep." Her voice gave nothing away.

Brianna and Shay were also in the room. They grinned at Kent then quickly ushered everyone else out. Now that his prayers had come true, Kent didn't know what to say, where to begin.

"Well? *Are* you my fiancé?" she asked, one haughty eyebrow arched.

"If you want me," he whispered. Kent moved to her bed, touched her cheek then grasped her hands in his. "I love you. I've been an idiot, which you already know, but I love you, Jaclyn."

She didn't smile, she didn't laugh with joy. Instead big tears filled her gorgeous eyes and trickled down her cheeks.

"Don't cry, darling. Please don't cry." He edged onto the bed so he could fold her slight body into his arms. "You don't have to say anything. You don't have to do anything. Just be well. Be happy."

"I am happy." She pushed back to peer into his eyes. "Or I will be if you'll kiss me."

He hesitated. She'd been so ill. She'd been unconscious for days. What if he hurt her? What if—

"You're not scared, are you, Kent?" she asked, her beautiful eyes sparkling.

"Always," he said seriously. "But I'm learning how to give

that to God. He's in charge now." He whispered a prayer of thanksgiving then leaned forward and kissed Hope's favorite pediatrician as he'd longed to for weeks, pouring his heart and soul into their embrace.

Jaclyn kept her arms around his neck when he pulled away, her eyes closed.

"What are you doing?" he asked, brushing his fingers over her lovely face.

"I'm going back to sleep so I can savor this dream," she murmured.

"This is no dream." He gave her arm a gentle squeeze. "I need you wide awake, my darling doctor. We have plans to make."

"Plans? What plans?"

"For starters, we're going to get married. In the church in Hope. Since you're in charge of renovations there, you'd better get busy because I'm not waiting long to make you Mrs. McCloy. Or is it Dr. Mrs. McCloy?"

"You haven't even asked me yet," Jaclyn teased.

A stern-faced nurse entered the room. Kent winked at the love of his life.

"I'm waiting till you get out of here. Then I'll do it properly. But I figured you could start making plans since you're just lazing around here." He kissed her but more medical personnel arrived and the nurse ordered Kent to leave the room.

He sat in the hall for an extended time.

That was okay. He had his own plans to make, his own thanks to give.

Oblivious to the comings and goings in the hall, Kent let the wonder of his answer to prayer, the joy of freedom from his worries and fears and the satisfaction of God's amazing grace flood his soul. The future was his and Jaclyn's, full of promise, waiting for them to discover what God had in store.

Saying thanks hardly seemed enough. But he said it over and over to the One who had given him a new beginning.

A month later, with a clean bill of health, Jaclyn left Hope with no clue about Kent's plans for this impromptu picnic. But she gladly relinquished all control and followed him over the hills on Tangay, every part of her being singing with happiness. Kent loved her. That's all she needed. She was happy to leave the rest in God's hands.

They arrived at the glade just as the sun began slowly sinking behind the hilltops. Glimmers of light illuminated the dusky area thanks to tiny solar lights Kent had planted in strategic places. A quilt lay spread on the ground flanked by candles waiting to be lit. Someone had strewn masses of wildflowers all over the grassy site. In the brook, jars filled with fireflies were tethered to the shore. They twinkled and glowed, chasing away the gloom. The heat of summer gave way to peaceful, tranquil coolness.

Kent helped Jaclyn dismount, not missing the chance to envelop her in his arms and kiss her. Jaclyn reveled in his embrace and kissed him back, wondering if there was any medical evidence to support her suspicion that women in her situation could melt from sheer happiness.

Kent led her to the old bench he'd built and hovered solicitously until she was seated. Her heart boomed in her ears when he knelt in front of her.

"Dr. Jaclyn LaForge, I love you more than anything else in this world. You challenge me and make me a stronger, better person. You give me hope and strength and confidence. Most of all you give me courage to leave the past behind and trust God for the future. You are my future. I want to share each moment with you. Will you marry me?"

She took a moment to savor the beauty of his words. Then she spoke the words she'd held inside for so long.

"I love you, Kent. You're a precious gift from God." She touched his cheek, grazing her fingers across his skin and reveling in the love that welled inside. Her throat clogged for a moment and she fought to gain control. "I can never thank you enough for getting the clinic finished. I thought that was my heart's desire yet you showed me God had more in store for me. So much more. Because of you I learned I was worthy of love, that I didn't have to earn it. Yes, I will marry you, I love you."

"Then this is my pledge to you." He slid a ring onto her finger, a gorgeous sapphire the exact shade of his eyes, flanked by two glittering diamonds. He kissed the ring in place then cupped her face in his hands so he could enjoy the love glowing in her eyes. "I was afraid we'd never have this time, afraid you'd never hear me tell you how much I love you. I've wasted a lot of time being afraid." He smoothed a hand over her gleaming hair, his fingertips trailing down the strands until they rested against the pulse in her neck. "I will never forget how empty my life seemed when I thought you wouldn't be there. Nothing else seemed to matter because you fill my world, Jaclyn. You make me hope and dream. I'm going to trust God and take on whatever challenges He sends. With your help, I'll replace fear with hope."

As she relished the pure bliss of the moment, Jaclyn's thoughts went to her sister. Jessica had brought Jaclyn to Hope, to this man and his precious love.

She savored the feel of Kent's arms around her, his lips on hers. When Kent finally drew back from her, he was as breathless as she.

Jaclyn thought she could sit there forever.

Until her stomach growled.

"Come on, it's time I fed you." Laughing, he took her hand and drew her to the quilt. He'd brought skewers of chicken, golden brown potatoes—the first of the season—and fresh asparagus. And last but not least, tiny, succulent wild straw-berries he'd picked from his mother's garden.

"Thank you, darling," Jaclyn said when she was replete with food and love.

He touched his lips to hers then leaned back. "When can we get married?"

"Heddy is my second in command on the church restora-tion and she's insistent that everything will be done by Sep-tember. She's chosen the first Saturday of the month. Is that soon enough?" She couldn't resist tracing his eyebrows, ca-ressing his cheek, smoothing her fingers over his smiling mouth.

"Heddy chose our wedding day?" He frowned.

"Well, she insists on being our wedding planner." Once Kent had stopped laughing, Jaclyn filled him in on the details Heddy had already arranged. "And by the way, both Mom and Dad will be walking me down the aisle. Then they're going on a second honeymoon cruise. They've certainly mended their relationship." She studied him, anxious about his lack of response. "What's wrong?"

"Nothing. I just hope I can get the ranch sold before Sep-tember."

"Oh." Jaclyn tried to hide her smile. "Well, you won't."

"Oh." He lifted a quizzical eyebrow. "How do you know that?"

"Heddy's put the word out that the ranch is officially off the market. According to her you and I need the ranch to raise our kids properly and Hope needs a petting zoo and animal sanctuary to bring in tourists." Jaclyn leaned forward and kissed his nose. "This time, my darling, I heartily agree with Heddy. You cannot sell the ranch. Our future is here." She waved a hand.

"But, sweetheart—"

"No buts. With God, all things are possible. Hey, maybe

we could use that on our wedding invitations. What do you think?"

Kent could think of nothing but kissing his beautiful fiancée.

Epilogue

"I've never seen a lovelier September day." Brianna waited until Jaclyn's father had helped Jaclyn out of the car. Then she straightened the bride's veil. "You look stunning. Such a simple dress and yet it's so gorgeous."

"Thank you. Both of you look amazing." Jaclyn was relieved her friends loved the red bridesmaid dresses Heddy had sewn. "It won't be too much for you—going through this with Zac as best man?"

"It would happen sooner or later once I start work in the clinic." She paused. "Zac and I will never get back what we once had. I've accepted that." Brianna's words sounded airy and carefree but a furrow creased her brow.

Never say never, Jaclyn wanted to say. But she didn't. She'd given up trying to control the world. Now she prayed for her friends and left the rest up to God.

"And you, Shay? Are you all right with Nick as Kent's groomsman?"

"Nick and I have been friends forever. I hope we'll have time after the wedding to catch up." The former model smiled her much-photographed grin. "And soon I also hope I'll be moving back to Hope, too."

"Great! Whispering Hope clinic is ready and waiting for both of you."

"Come along now, dears. It's time this bride saw her groom." Heddy ushered them up the stairs to the church, signaled the organist and handed out the bouquets.

Her heart full, Jaclyn took her parents' arms and followed her dearest friends up the aisle of the old church in Hope to the man who held her heart. The church wasn't finished, not even close. But tons of flowers culled from the gardens of Hope-ites filled the tiny sanctuary to overflowing and hid the imperfections.

The townspeople were all there, squeezed into pews, standing in the balcony. They came because this was *their* doctor and *their* vet and it was up to them to make sure the wedding day went off without a hitch.

Jaclyn's gaze locked on Kent after she'd taken the first step, and stayed there. She saw joy and pride and a host of other emotions rush across his face. But mostly she saw love. When her parents placed her hand in his, she sent a prayer of thanksgiving heavenward.

The ceremony went off without a hitch. Their kiss sealed their promises to each other and then they walked down the aisle of the church, husband and wife. Outside, the people of Hope showered them with a blizzard of rice and good wishes.

Kent escorted Jaclyn into a horse-drawn carriage. A second carriage followed with the attendants. After photographs they returned to the church and the garden reception Heddy had arranged behind the church.

"Are you sure it was a good idea to let her do this?" Kent asked as he helped Jaclyn down.

"I had to, you know that." Jaclyn grimaced. "Being the only doctor in town didn't allow much time for planning a reception. I'm glad we found a locum for the clinic. I refuse to give up my honeymoon."

"You know you would in an instant. And I'd be right by your side." He folded her hand over his arm. "Let's go see what Heddy's created."

What Heddy had created was a flower-filled garden scene with tables scattered across the grass.

"It's beautiful, Heddy." Jaclyn embraced the woman who'd help her find her place in Hope.

"We all worked on it, as a town should. You and Kent have given us our town back. You've helped us heal the rift that threatened to destroy us. Now it's your time for each other." She led them to a table where the attendants already sat. "We love you, Doctors McCloy and LaForge."

As she and Kent enjoyed the reception specially prepared for them, Jaclyn studied the assembly with a full heart.

"What's wrong, darling?" Kent whispered when she borrowed his handkerchief to wipe away a tear.

"I'm just full of blessings," Jaclyn said, snuggling next to him. "You, my parents, my best friends, Hope—my life is full of joy." She paused a moment, studying him. "I'm so glad I came here to start Jessica's clinic. My sister told me to live my life and trust God. She was so smart."

"Yes, she was. Because it all starts with God, doesn't it?" He pressed his lips to hers. "Together we'll pass on Jessica's words and let God use us to reach others. Deal?"

"Deal for a lifetime," she agreed.

Then the minister led all of Hope in a prayer of blessing for the new couple.

* * * * *

Dear Reader,

I hope you enjoyed this first installment of my newest miniseries for Love Inspired. Jaclyn and Kent had a past in common and problems both thought too big to resolve until they came together and let God heal their hearts. I can't wait for you to meet their friends, Zac and Brianna in the next book in the Healing Hearts miniseries, *Yuletide Proposal,* coming in December 2012.

Can you believe Love Inspired has been around for fifteen years? I remember so well that very first story I wrote for Love Inspired and how delighted I was to finally be writing the kind of books I like to read, stories with hope and joy, stories that included a spiritual message. Now we've expanded, grown up as it were, so that we have three separate lines of Love Inspired stories—so much good reading. And I'm still here! Fifteen years and thirty-four stories later I can only say thanks to a wonderful team of editors, publicity and promotion, artists and all the gifted folks who've helped make each one of my Love Inspired books better. My deepest thanks to all of you. You are amazing, blessings from heaven.

And thank you to you, dear reader. Thank you for fifteen years of generous cards, sweet letters and delightful emails that encourage me as I seek to write God's stories. Thank you for your patience and understanding and for your faithfulness to our wonderful line of books. I wish you peace, my friend; the calm certainty that God is alive and working with you, in you and for you. I wish you joy—richer, deeper, far above and beyond anything you've ever felt before. Most of all, I wish you love, the kind of impossible, unbelievable, enduring love God waits to shower on you if you will but ask Him.

Until next time.

Blessings,

Lois Richer

Discussion Questions

1. As a teen, Jaclyn lost her twin sister. Do you know any teens who have suffered a loss? How did it affect their lives?

2. Jaclyn dealt with her tragedy by lashing out and damaging property which alienated much of the townspeople. How can we help others in situations like Jaclyn's deal with their pain appropriately?

3. Kent blamed himself for causing his wife's death. This affected the way he viewed his future goals and plans. Are there experiences in your past which have shaped your expectations of God's ability to use you or to make your life fulfilling? Note ways we may mistake God's plans for our own thoughts.

4. Heddy Grange appeared in the story as a problem but eventually became a liaison to both Jaclyn and Kent. Consider people you know, like Heddy, who cause problems because they don't know how to help. What changes could you make to help them find their niche?

5. Jaclyn thought she could earn God's favor if she just tried hard enough, did enough. How does grace fit in? Is it enough to accept grace and do nothing? How can one find balance?

6. Kent was very active in town, but his activity was primarily driven by fear. Discuss whether this is a bad thing, or whether we need something to motivate us to begin

making a difference where we live. Is there relevance for you in Kent's actions?

7. Kent was impressed by the Bible's story of David and his relationship with God as noted in the Psalms. Describe themes you've noted in these psalms. What makes them unique to this man and how can we, in this era, apply what David knew and spoke about?

8. Jaclyn felt she could never regain the trust of those whom she'd hurt. Discuss appropriate ways to deal with such events using real situations that have happened in your world.

9. Kent did everything in his physical power to make his world right but eventually felt the only solution was to leave Hope. Do you understand his motivation? If you think his view was skewed, what alternative do you see?

10. At the end of the story, the rebuilding of Hope's church is not finished but Jaclyn and Kent get married anyway. Consider the significance of this.

A COWBOY'S PROMISE
Linda Ford

Chapter One

Buffalo Hollow, Dakota Territory, 1884

He rode into the tiny town, pulling his hat low over his face. It wasn't likely anyone here knew him but he wasn't taking a chance. He wouldn't have stopped—just kept riding north until he reached Canada, someplace deep in the mountains where no one would ever find him—but he was out of supplies. A man could get mighty hungry living on rabbit cooked over a low fire.

He swung from his horse in front of the general store— Tate's Mercantile—checking both ways up and down the dusty streets of Buffalo Hollow, Dakota Territory. Would the sense of being followed ever leave him? Even in the wilds of the Rockies. He shivered in the cold wind. It threatened snow. The lateness of the season was another reason for urgency.

He stepped into the store and immediately sensed that something was wrong. He noticed two rough, dirty men leaning against the counter. The woman at the till looked cautious but not frightened, though, so he held back, waiting to see if he should proceed or slip away.

"Come on, missee. We only want to have us a good time. You can surely 'commodate us." It was the taller of the pair, a man with hair like an overgrown porcupine and stubble to match.

The younger, shorter one with a nasty leer chortled.

"I'll get your supplies, but then I'm asking you to be on your way." The pretty young thing spoke as calm as could be, even though he noticed that she clung to the far edge of the space behind the counter.

"We ain't in no rush, is we, Stook?" The younger man had a rusty-hinge voice.

Holt edged closer, unnoticed by the pair. He figured by the way the gal's eyelids flickered that she'd seen him and was preparing to deal with *three* rowdies. Well, he'd soon put her mind at ease about that. Holt wasn't another troublemaker—though some claimed otherwise.

He was about to provide his own suggestion that the pair move along when a tiny voice whispered from a nearby doorway. "Lizzie, can I come out now?"

The drifters jerked upright. Stook grinned wickedly. "Lookee here, a little doll. I betcha she'd like to play with us, wouldn't you, darlin'?"

Lizzie, the child had called the woman behind the counter. Seemed to suit her—all feisty and fiery eyed as she sprang toward the blue-eyed youngster. "Emma, I told you to stay with Pa."

Pa? Where was her father? Why wasn't he out here taking care of this pair of ruffians?

Stook moved with the sly quickness of a snake and grabbed tiny Emma's arm before Lizzie could reach her. "Now let's negotiate something more fun. You—" he pointed at Lizzie "—start being 'commodating. Or—" He jerked the child's arm.

Emma cried out, her sky-blue eyes wide as a bucket.

"That sounds fair, doesn't it, Joe?"

Holt had had enough. He stepped forward. "Don't sound

fair to me. Two big men picking on two girls. Didn't your mother teach you better?"

The pair spun around as if struck by lightning. Just as fast, Joe pulled out a gun.

Holt was unarmed, but the gun didn't scare him half as bad as it should have. *Lord, looks like we'll be meeting face-to-face soon. Might as well die this way as from a hangman's noose.*

Chapter Two

Lizzie didn't know who the tall, dark stranger was. Nor if he was ultimately bad news. But unless the Good Lord gave her the strength to act quickly, he was about to die.

Emma thankfully escaped Stook's clutches and scurried back to Pa as the two rowdies remained intent on the stranger for the moment. It was all she needed. Lizzie made one quick movement.

"All right. Put your gun down." She leveled a shotgun at Joe, whose eyes fair bugged out of his head when he turned to stare at her. "Don't think I won't use this because I have in the past." Once. When she'd shot a wild dog she feared would attack Emma. But she would use it against this pair if push came to shove.

Joe swallowed hard and gaped at her.

"Best do as the lady says," the stranger drawled. "Pretty sure she means business."

"And if you don't think so, you better reconsider." Pa, his voice surprisingly strong, suddenly stood at her side, a pistol in his hands.

Lizzie didn't shift a fraction, but out of the corner of her eyes she noted it took both hands for Pa to hold the gun steady.

Joe slid his firearm to the counter and backed away, his

hands above his head. Stook shuffled at his side, a look on his face of pure disgust.

The stranger held the door for them and let it hit their heels on the way out. "If that don't beat all." He roared with laughter.

My, but the man had a rolling, gut-pleasing way of laughing. It made her want to join in his amusement. Made her feel all sweet and pleased. Their gazes connected with a great jolt of something she didn't recognize, couldn't name, and yet it echoed with dreams she only allowed herself late at night.

Pa still held his gun level. "You, too, mister."

She tore her attention from the man causing her heart to dip strangely. "No, Pa. He wasn't with them."

"How can you be sure? Identify yourself, stranger."

"Holt Perry, sir. I just happened by. Needing some supplies." He regarded Pa, letting the older man assess him.

Lizzie wondered what Pa saw. A tall, lean man with eyes like warm campfire coffee? Eyes that seemed to blare caution and humor at the same time. Did he notice the man's hands? So big and strong. The kind that would control wild horses just as skillfully as sweep a woman off her feet.

If a woman were so inclined, which she wasn't. She was committed to being mother to Emma and helper to her father.

"Where you hail from, Holt Perry?" Pa was clearly not about to take the man at face value.

"No place in particular."

"Then where you be going?"

"North. Thought I'd try life in Canada."

Pa grunted. "Sounds like a man running from something."

Holt Perry didn't answer.

Pa lowered the gun, let it hang from his right hand. "Lizzie, fill the man's order so he can be on his way."

"Yes, Pa."

She stuck the shotgun behind the counter just as Pa moaned and crashed to the floor.

Chapter Three

Holt saw Mr. Tate's eyes roll up into his head. Holt sprang forward but not quickly enough to keep the other man from folding into a heap on the oiled wooden floor. Holt reached his side at the same moment as Lizzie. They bumped into each other, backed away. Embarrassment fluttered through her eyes and then she turned to kneel at her father's side. "Pa." She nudged his arm. "Pa."

Holt pushed aside a rush of wishes. Life would never include the things a man wanted—home, a woman to smile in greeting as he walked in the door. Not while he was a hunted man. But the alternative was to face biased justice. His false accusers had left no doubt in anyone's mind that Holt was guilty. Not that a soul had been looking to defend his innocence.

He knelt beside Lizzie, studying the inert man. "He's passed out." He shoved one arm under Mr. Tate's shoulders and the other under his knees, grunting as he lifted him. "Show me to his bed."

Lizzie considered the request for barely a second before she nodded. "Right this way." She led him to the doorway that Emma had scampered through such a short time ago and into their tiny living quarters. It was as cold as a barn in the cramped room.

"The fire's gone out," he observed.

She nodded and led him to a narrow cot in the corner. The covers were rumpled. "Emma, come out of there. Pa needs the bed."

The quilts wiggled like a worm and Emma emerged, her light brown hair a tangled crown. "I's trying to keep warm."

"Crawl into our bed." Lizzie tipped her head toward the narrow loft at the other end.

"It's cold. Pa had this one warm."

Lizzie smoothed her hands over Emma's hair. "You'll have to make the bed warm yourself. Now scoot."

But Emma stayed close by, shivering despite the layers of sweaters she wore.

Holt lowered their father to the bed, thinking that he was far too light for a man of his frame. And he understood why Emma liked her father's bed. The man was fevered. Holt got him comfortable then stepped away for Lizzie and Emma to hover at his side.

"Pa, wake up." Lizzie rubbed his wrists and patted his cheeks.

"How long has he been ill?" Holt asked.

"Long time," Emma said, her little face wreathed in worry. "Is he gonna die?"

"Of course not." Lizzie's voice dared such a thing to happen.

Mr. Tate moaned. Saw Lizzie. "You're safe."

"Yes, Pa. I'm safe. So is Emma."

"I should…" His voice drifted into blankness.

"He needs something hot to drink." Holt looked about for firewood. Saw three sticks in the box and a lump of coal. "Show me the woodpile and coal shed and I'll get some heat into this place."

Lizzie rose slowly and faced him. In the depths of her violet eyes he read regret and determination. "We haven't enough fuel to keep both fires going." She meant the stove in the store as well as the cookstove in the living quarters.

Holt realized Mr. Tate had been ill long enough to cut into their winter store.

The man signaled Holt to draw closer. Holt did so, bending low to catch Mr. Tate's softly spoken words. "I'm too ill to care for my girls." He tried to lift his hand to grasp Holt's shirt but lacked the strength. "Mr. Perry, you seem a decent man. Promise me you'll stay and help them prepare for the cold weather."

Holt knew then and there that God had spared his life for one purpose. He would trust God to protect him from his pursuers while he achieved it. "I promise, I'll help."

He had two days' advantage on the men on his trail—three at the most—but now he had given his word and whatever the risk to himself, he would help these people.

Chapter Four

Lizzie heard the stranger pledge to help her family. It would be a relief, but Lizzie wouldn't acknowledge how desperately they needed his charity.

"We'll manage," she said to him. Hadn't God promised to take care of them? She clung to the idea. Otherwise her legs would buckle at the thought of how fast the coal pile had been depleted. "Pa is improving every day."

She spoke more from stubborn determination than truth, but she was uneasy about a stranger hanging around. Even one who had defended her and carried her father gently to his bed. She turned from Pa and Holt. "I'll tend to your order now."

"Lizzie." Pa's weak voice brought her back to his side. She knelt so she could hear his words. "I prayed for help. I have to believe this is God's answer."

Although his words were but a whisper she knew when she glanced up at Holt that he'd heard them. Again Holt's gaze was riveted to hers. Silently saying he wanted only to help.

She longed to believe it. But her natural caution warned her to be careful.

"Ma'am, at least let me get the chill off this place. I won't use any more of your wood and coal than necessary. And if you'd be so kind as to share your meal, I'll sleep in the livery station tonight. Tomorrow…" He pulled at his lip as if considering his options.

Even as she considered hers. She had precious few.

"I'd be pleased to make sure you have a fair stock of fuel. Might take me more'n a day, though. If that's a problem…?"

Emma stood shivering at the foot of Pa's bed. Lizzie ached to give her little sister the warmth of home and the security Lizzie had known when she was six. Instead she had only a cold room to offer. Trying to run the store and care for everything left her scant time to play mother to her sister.

It was the look of hope on Emma's face that made up Lizzie's mind.

"I'll feed you and provide your travel supplies in exchange for a winter's store of fuel."

Holt grinned. "It's a deal."

He offered his hand to make it official. Lizzie hesitated, suspecting that she might regret this agreement as much as she needed it.

Slowly she lifted her hand to his, let him grip it. Solid. Strong. She withdrew her hand. Couldn't decide what to do with it. Press it to her waist? Wrap her other hand around it and share the heat? In the end, she unnecessarily tidied a lock of hair, tucking it into her bun.

He rubbed his palms together. "First things first. Let's get a fire going and make this room cozy."

Emma followed him to the cold stove. "We're going to be warm?"

"Soon, little Emma. Very soon. And I'll make sure you've got enough fuel that you can be snug as a bug all winter."

Emma gave him a smile full of sweet trust. "I think I like you."

He grinned at the girl. "What's not to like?" He shared the smile with Lizzie, and she felt as if the sun had dawned in her chest. It frightened her.

"A man from no place. On his way north. Not the sort of man to like too much, Emma." Lizzie warned herself as much as her little sister.

Chapter Five

"*A man from no place. On his way north. Not the sort of man to like too much, Emma.*"

Holt recognized Lizzie's caution for what it was—a warning to her little sister to remember this was temporary. He wished he could assure her it was misplaced. But it wasn't. For his own safety he had to keep moving.

But for now, he intended to honor his promise to Mr. Tate. The door to the store opened and Lizzie slipped away. The fire began to thaw out the room. "I'm going to see about more fuel," he told Emma and stepped outside. There was only enough wood for a month or less, he thought as he examined the woodpile. He moved to the coal shed. A small heap in the middle of the floor. No wonder Lizzie was rationing it so tightly. It would take him more than a few days to provide a winter's supply. Might even take a week. He grinned. Didn't seem such a bad prospect.

Then he thought of his pursuers, just days behind him. He rubbed at his throat at the specter of being caught and taken back. Holt shrugged off the thought. He had given his word, and he wouldn't break his promise.

He chopped wood for kindling then filled a coal bucket and carried it inside. But Holt drew to an abrupt halt as he entered the living quarters. The room glowed with hominess. A pot simmered on the stove, filling the air with a pleasant aroma. Mr. Tate reclined on his pillows as Lizzie helped him drink from a cup. Emma sat cross-legged at the foot of the bed, playing with a doll.

The scene filled him with sharp regret; a man on the run could never enjoy such pleasures. But this temporary taste was a gift from God. He would enjoy every minute of it and cherish the memory in the future. "It smells like home in here."

Lizzie glanced up. "I just made tea. Do you want a cupful?"

"Sounds good. I'll get it." But by the time he hung his hat and shucked out of his coat, she had placed a steaming cup on the table for him. "Thanks."

Emma sat across from him. "Where's your home?"

Holt felt Lizzie and her pa's silent interest in his answer. "Used to be Ohio. Before my pa died."

"My ma died, too."

"I'm sorry. But you got your pa and your sister."

She nodded, her eyes bright. "They love me."

"What's not to love?"

She giggled at his question. Then tipped her head to study him more. "So why didn't you stay with your ma?"

"I did some, until she married again. My stepfather didn't much like having a sixteen-year-old boy hanging about. So I left."

"Aww. That's sad."

He let her mull it over as he sipped tea that cheered his insides.

"So where you going now?"

"Nowhere in particular."

"Then how do you know you aren't there already?"

Emma's innocent question hung in the air. Holt couldn't tell her that staying wasn't safe, no matter how much he might want to. He had no wish for them to get mixed up in his troubles. Regret boiled through his insides, scalding them with loneliness and desperation. "I just know."

Chapter Six

Lizzie heard the longing in Emma's voice. Understood it. With Holt there, the room was warmer and more secure than it had been since Pa fell ill in the summer. But Holt wasn't the answer they needed…although she couldn't deny the deep gratitude and relief she felt at his offer to make sure they had enough coal and wood to get them through winter.

Pa indicated he'd had enough tea and she moved to the stove to stir the soup. Rationing fuel had meant restricting her cooking to what she could prepare on the pot-bellied stove in the store. But now she'd be able to make better meals. Surely Pa would then start to improve.

She studied him. He seemed to be resting peacefully. Praise the Good Lord.

Her eyes continued on to Holt. Emma had brought out her rag doll and was chattering to him about "Miss Ellen's" adventures. Holt nodded and made appropriate comments, appearing to take the child's imaginations seriously. Everything inside Lizzie tilted sideways at the sight of the big man bent close to Emma, his over-long black hair brushing his strong jawline.

He turned, noticed her watching and grinned. "Miss Ellen has been a busy young lady. She's visited several cities I haven't seen. Even been to the ocean." His coffee-colored eyes filled with amusement. And something more that drew her into her own dream world.

She found herself longing for things she would not allow herself to confess—a home such as she'd known as a child. Security. Love. She gave a mental snort. Not that she wasn't loved. But that wasn't the sort of love she meant. In the most secret places of her heart, she yearned for a love that cherished her as a woman.

But her responsibility to her pa and little sister made such romantic notions impossible. The few men who had shown any interest in Lizzie had made it plain they didn't want to be tied down by her family.

She jerked her attention back to the simmering pot. Her imagination was almost as rampant as Emma's. "The soup is ready. Emma, would you set the table?"

"Okay. Holt, you hold Miss Ellen."

Lizzie expected the man to protest. When he didn't she had to steal a look. He sat with Miss Ellen on his lap, his big hands cradling the rag doll as gingerly as if it were china. Try as she might she couldn't contain a chortle.

Holt grinned at her. "It's a rare occasion that I get to hold someone's best friend."

Their gazes locked. Did she see interest in his eyes, or was it only her own hopes she saw? She tore her eyes away.

He was a stranger. She couldn't possibly have feelings for him in such a short time. Yes, he was kind to help them, but he was only passing through. Likely, as Pa said, on the run. She'd had enough of young men who had only leaving on their minds, who expected she should abandon her family to join their wild pursuits. This man was no different. The sooner he moved on, the better, she decided as she began to ladle out the soup.

He waited until she sat down. "Do you want me to say

grace?" At her nod, he did so. He spoke as if he and God were on a friendly basis.

Which was no reason to allow herself even a thread of attraction. Words easier said than obeyed.

Chapter Seven

"How long do you think it will take to restock our coal and wood?" Lizzie asked him.

Holt tasted the soup, stalling. "It's been a long time since I enjoyed anything this good—might be a good while before you have enough fuel," he teased.

His response was an evasion, but Holt had no intention of answering her question about how long he'd be around. Somehow he couldn't bear the thought of how she would look at him once she found out he was a wanted man. But if it weren't for his pursuers, he'd be tempted to stay the winter.

Emma giggled. "It's only soup. We eat it a lot."

"How fortunate for you. Sure beats fricassee rabbit." He smiled at Lizzie. "'Preciate your inviting me for supper."

She laughed, easing the tension that scraped along his nerves at the way she shied away from meeting his glance. "Seems you invited yourself."

"Are you insinuating I'm not welcome?" He put his spoon down in mock protest.

Emma almost jumped from her chair. "No, she didn't meant that, did you, Lizzie?" The girl's eyes grew wide, pleading. "Say you aren't going."

But he kept his gaze on Lizzie, silently demanded a response from her.

"Calm down, Emma. Of course he's welcome."

Holt grinned, far more on the inside than the out. The admission had cost Lizzie a dose of pride but he decided it was worth it.

"So tell me about Buffalo Hollow." He listened keenly as they described the frontier town and the people living nearby. The information might prove valuable should someone come hunting him. And he knew they would. They were on his trail even now. He could only pray something would delay them.

They finished the soup. While Lizzie washed the dishes, Holt insisted on drying them. "I do my share," he said when she would have refused his help.

"Very well." There was a shrug in her voice, but he caught a flash of something in her eyes that made him think she wasn't as indifferent as she pretended. He allowed himself a bit of joy, a moment of dreaming, before he pushed reality to the fore.

"Emma," Lizzie said, "Get ready for bed."

Emma looked ready to argue then sighed like a martyr and climbed the ladder to the loft. "It's nice and warm up here."

Mr. Tate had slept through the meal, but as Holt dried the last bowl, he stirred. "Lizzie?" His frail voice barely reached the stove.

Lizzie hurried to him. "I'll get your soup right away, Pa."

"Wait."

She hovered at his side as he struggled to find words and the strength to say them.

"Is he still here?"

Holt moved to the bed. "I'm still here. I'll stay until there is enough fuel for the winter." Had he forgotten Holt's promise or did the man need something more? "Is there anything else?"

"Lizzie will give you money for the coal. Borrow the wagon from the livery man. He'll direct you to the nearest coal mine."

"I'll do so." He waited but Mr. Tate seemed to have nothing more to say.

Lizzie brought a bowl of soup and pulled a chair close to feed her father.

Emma climbed down the ladder, Miss Ellen tucked under her arm and a book in one hand. Seeing that her sister was busy, she turned her attention to Holt. "Will you read me my story?"

Her question jolted through his insides. He sucked in air and tried not to see the room—cheery, full of love and family. Everything he wanted, and now because of the lies about him, could never have.

Chapter Eight

Lizzie saw the way Holt's mouth grew flat. Sensed a stiffening of his spine. Bad enough Emma demanded he hold her doll. Now to ask him to read her a story…

"Emma, don't bother him. I'll read to you as soon as I'm done with Pa."

Holt shuddered so slightly she would have missed it if she hadn't been looking carefully. "Not a bother." He reached for the book.

Emma took his hand and led him to the rocking chair that had once been Ma's. The girl waited for him to sit then indicated she had to perch on his knee.

Lizzie watched anxiously, torn between allowing her sister this pleasure and wanting to protect her from a man who would walk out of their lives as suddenly as he'd walked in. Someone they knew next to nothing about. But she remembered how she'd sat on Pa's knee as he read to her. How could she deny her little sister this simple happiness? So Lizzie only observed, prepared to intervene if needed.

Holt pulled Emma to his chest, allowed her to snuggle close, and read from the Bible storybook.

Lizzie's eyes stung as she blinked away tears. She would not cry even though the scene reminded her of all she'd lost.

And Emma, too. She concentrated on helping Pa get settled for the night.

After a while, Holt stopped reading. Lizzie glanced over at them and saw that Emma had fallen asleep.

She kissed her father's forehead and went to her sister. "Emma, honey, time for bed." She bent over to pick Emma up, bringing her so close to Holt she could see the flecks of gold in his irises, feel the heat from his body, inhale the scent of wood and wide spaces from his skin. She tried to pull back but was caught in a net of longing and loneliness.

Emma stirred and Lizzie jumped away. "Come along." She escorted her sister to the ladder, made sure she climbed up safely and crawled under the covers. Miss Ellen rested on her cheek as Emma sighed and slept.

Slowly Lizzie turned, finding Holt watching her. Her breath stalled halfway up her throat at the intensity of his gaze. She couldn't move. Couldn't tear herself from that look.

He jerked to his feet. "I'll bid you good night." He grabbed his coat, slammed his hat on his head and reached for the doorknob. Then he paused. She felt the air stiffen between them. "Ma'am." He pivoted to face her. "I thank you for your hospitality."

"You'll be back for breakfast?" she asked, hoping she didn't sound half as desperate as she felt about his answer.

"I…can't say. I may go to the mine early. Good night," he said again and left without looking back.

Chapter Nine

It took the better part of a day to go to the coal mine and return. This was his third trip. Holt welcomed the reprieve. Almost as much as he minded it.

In spite of himself, he'd been drawn back to the cozy little room for breakfast with Lizzie, Emma and Mr. Tate. It was sweet agony, reminding him of the kind of life he would never enjoy.

Now, as he huddled on the wagon seat, shrugged up inside his coat against the cold wind, he decided to focus on things he was happy about rather than the things he couldn't have.

Mr. Tate was still too weak to get out of bed on his own but decidedly stronger than the first day, when he'd collapsed on the floor. This morning he had sat up in bed and fed himself.

Lizzie hadn't been able to stop smiling. "He's made a turn for the better," she'd remarked.

"I 'spect it will take a few days for him to regain his strength."

"I know, but it's been so long since he fed himself."

Holt had allowed himself to squeeze her shoulder briefly. "I'm glad. For all of you."

She'd leaned into his touch. Or had he only wished that? Dreamt it? He comforted himself with the assurance that there had been no mistaking the flash of gratitude in her eyes. Whether for his encouragement or her father's improvement he couldn't guess. But he could hope it was partly the former. Yes, it was definitely a good thing he had several all-day trips to make.

Yet every day meant those who hunted him were that much closer. They should have overtaken him by now. He pretended he didn't feel the fear boiling through his insides. God must have intervened in some way in order to allow Holt this respite.

Dark shadows already filled the hollows as he headed down the lone street of Buffalo Hollow toward the store. The wind had increased in intensity, bringing with it the smell of snow.

He studied each doorway, each lamp-lit window carefully, letting his breath whistle past his teeth when he saw no one that made him think he should leave in a hurry.

God in heaven, You see how this family needs help. I'm more than prepared to lend it, but I'm trusting You to hold the bad weather and my pursuers off until I can cross the forty-ninth.

He pulled up to the coal shed, backed the wagon as close as he could and began to shovel the coal inside. Once he finished, he returned the horse and wagon to the livery barn. The man on duty seemed bored, and Holt saw an opportunity to get some information. "Anyone coming and going today?" He kept the tension from his voice and hoped the man would think his question only idle conversation.

"Nope. Most people got the good sense to stay home with snow threatening."

"'Spect that's so." His mind somewhat at ease, Holt hurried to the store, entering through the rear door that he had repaired.

He smiled as Emma ran to him. "You're back."

"Yup." His gaze shifted to Lizzie and his heart soared at her smile of welcome.

"Feels like snow. Glad you got here before it comes."

"Me, too." Except…he should be riding north ahead of the snow. He dare not get trapped here for the winter—they'd find him for sure. Holt could practically feel the noose around his neck. But he had given his word to Mr. Tate that he'd make sure this family was prepared for the cold weather, and not even the fear of hanging would make him leave before he'd done that.

Chapter Ten

Holt stayed until Emma went to bed then he went out into the winter. To sleep at the livery barn. Lizzie shivered. The house grew colder when he left, and she admitted it wasn't simply because of the draft coming in the door. His presence lit the room. Perhaps that's why Pa was improving. That and having a fire in the stove. Thank God Holt had shown up when he did.

Somehow they would manage when he left.

Lizzie shook away another shiver that had nothing to do with the temperature of the room. "Pa, do you need anything more?"

"I'm fine." He pulled the covers up to his chin and turned on his side. Like Holt said, it would take time for him to regain his strength.

She thought of joining Emma in the loft but she wasn't tired, so she sat at the table and tackled the mending. It was a mindless enough job that her thoughts drifted…straight to Holt and the way he made her feel. If only she had room in her life for the kind of dreams that he kindled. For the first time, she imagined how it would be to ride side by side with a man who cared for her. To be held and sheltered. To create a home for him.

But she had a little sister and sick father who needed her, not to mention a store to run. And he had never indicated he wanted to stay. Why just this morning she'd observed him staring out the window as if counting the minutes until he was on his way. No point in dwelling on things that could be different, or dreaming impossible dreams. With a heavy sigh, she put away the mending and headed for bed.

During the night the wind increased, rattling the door and windows, screaming around the corner of the house. She normally let the fire die down while they slept, but the wind sucked the warmth from the house and twice she climbed down the ladder to put more coal on the embers, hovering over the stove until the heat increased and then scurrying back to bed.

Sometime during the night, the sound of the wind changed, pulling Lizzie from her light sleep. She listened, trying to identify why it had wakened her. She realized the sound was coming from inside the house. She tensed, wishing she'd brought the shotgun to bed with her. Emma was curled up next to her safe and sound. Lizzie intended to keep her that way.

She slipped from her covers, silently pulled on a robe and edged toward the ladder. The sound came again. She waited, not breathing. If it was an intruder she had no weapon to defend herself and her loved ones with.

And Pa. Down there. Helpless.

She tipped her head to catch the source and location of the sound.

And then it hit her. She knew what it was. Fear leapt into her throat, and she slid down the ladder without touching any of the rungs.

Chapter Eleven

Holt hurried from the livery barn as the first blush of dawn pinkened the sky. The snow had held off but the wind had a bite that made a man wish for a cave to hunker down in. Or even more alluring…a nice warm house with a woman's welcoming smile.

Like the ones Lizzie gave.

He shrugged farther down into the protection of his coat as he hurried up the street. Didn't even bother to check to the right and the left for anyone interested in a lone cowboy.

He ducked into the living quarters behind the store. "Brr. That's a cold wind."

The silence at his greeting made him freeze in the act of taking off his coat. He turned. Emma sat at the table, fear blazing from her big eyes. Lizzie knelt by her father's bed, sponging his face and arms.

It didn't take Holt more than a glance to know the man was burning with fever. He tossed off his coat. "How long has he been like this?"

"He woke me last night shouting and rambling incoherently. I've been trying to get his fever down since."

Mr. Tate hollered and swung his arm. Lizzie ducked.

Holt sprang into action. "Throw back his covers. We have

to sponge him all over." He worked as he talked, pulling Mr. Tate's shirt over his head and slipping his arms out of his union suit. By rights they should remove the underwear on his lower body as well, but he figured the man wouldn't want his girls to see him that way.

"Get me more water." Lizzie scrambled to bring him a basin. Holt took the washcloth, dipped it into the basin and washed the man from the waist up, letting the water evaporate.

Emma edged closer. "Is he gonna die?"

"No." Holt and Lizzie answered as one. He saw the set of her jaw, knew she would fight to her last breath to save her father. "I'm at your side." He would fight just as hard as she.

She looked at him, her eyes filled with gratitude.

"You take care of Emma. I'll look after your pa. Between us, it'll be okay." He wanted to give her a hug, to offer her comfort, but he had no right.

Holt returned his attention to the older man. This was something he could do for Lizzie. No matter the cost, he would honor his promise to Mr. Tate. And he would not fail her. If he was found and captured, so be it. He prayed God would enable him to face his fate with dignity.

Chapter Twelve

Lizzie rubbed her neck, trying to ease the strain caused from bending over Pa most of the night. She tried to persuade Emma to eat something. But her sister was as worried as she. As she tidied up, she watched Holt caring for Pa. The man wasn't the least bit awkward at playing nurse. Oh, how she took comfort from his strength and encouragement. The night had been interminably long and lonesome.

She handed him some tea that he paused only a moment to down.

"I've been trying since you got here to express my gratitude to you," she murmured. "But the words don't ever seem like enough. I don't know what I would have done without you," she murmured. Heat crept up her neck and stung her cheeks.

His grin was fleeting. "Perhaps God sent me here to help you. You ever think of that?"

She didn't answer, but she smiled to acknowledge the kindness of the thought.

A little later…or was it a great deal later…she reached over and took the cloth from him. "There's soup and sandwiches ready. Go eat while I tend to him."

Holt hesitated then went to the table. He sat across from Emma. "Where's Miss Ellen?"

Lizzie wondered if he'd have any more success diverting Emma than she had.

"Still in bed," the girl answered.

"Bet she's tired of being there."

Emma sighed loudly. "She's a doll."

"Yesterday she was your best friend. How would you like it if your best friend forgot about you?"

Lizzie watched Emma consider Holt's words.

"I wouldn't like it." She scrambled from her chair and up the ladder so fast Lizzie feared for her safety.

"Emma, slow down."

But Emma practically slid down the ladder, Miss Ellen tucked under her arm. She returned to the table and sat Miss Ellen beside her plate. "There you go. I didn't forget you. Not for a minute."

Lizzie looked to Holt. He watched her. She couldn't pull her eyes away. Didn't want to, finding warmth and comfort in his eyes. The air between them seemed to shift and shimmer. She drank long and hard from the silent promises he offered before she turned back to care for Pa.

"If only his fever would break," she murmured.

Emma clutched her doll to her chest. "Miss Ellen is worried."

Holt scooped Emma into his arms and brought her to Lizzie's side. "You aren't alone."

Lizzie nodded. Holt was here; his presence helped her find courage.

"God is with us. Let's ask Him to heal your pa." Holt bowed his head. Emma followed his example, as did Lizzie after a moment, struck by the deep assurance of Holt's faith.

Holt prayed for Pa to get better. And for them to know how to help.

But hours later his condition didn't improve and Pa grew steadily weaker.

Chapter Thirteen

Holt lost track of the hours as he and Lizzie alternately sponged Mr. Tate or tried to amuse Emma, the tension in the room getting thicker as the day waned. Nothing had changed with the sick man. Except the fever was sucking the life from him. What would happen to the girls if their father died?

"Is there no doctor we can call?" Holt asked.

"The nearest doctor is two days away and said he could do little when we called for him the last time." Lizzie's voice creaked with worry. She pressed a hand to her mouth, stifling a sob.

Holt longed to take her hands and pull her close. Offer comfort and encouragement. And so much more. But a man on the run had nothing to offer.

"I've heard tales about a Métis woman out on Burke Edwards's ranch," she said. "They say she has herbs that help cure illnesses. Her name is Paquette."

"I'm going to find her." He'd already started pulling on his coat. "How do I get to this ranch?"

Lizzie shook her head. "It's threatening a storm. It's too late in the day to make it back before dark."

If he wasn't so worried about Mr. Tate and the cold ride ahead of him he might have cheered. She didn't want him to go. She was concerned about his safety. "I'll return with help." A man could ride many a mile, face snow, darkness, even men wanting to execute frontier justice if he knew a woman waited for him.

Not allowing himself a chance to examine the foolishness of such thoughts, he strode out into the dark and out of town. As he rode from town, the wind tore his breath away but it didn't deter him. He kept up a steady pace until he reached a set of buildings that he hoped was the ranch he sought. His limbs stiff with cold, he dismounted and staggered to the door. His knock was answered by a dark-haired man. "I'm looking for a woman named Paquette."

A bent-over, crippled woman stood near the stove. "I be Paquette, me. Who you?"

He explained about Mr. Tate's illness. "We heard you could help."

She nodded. "I have cures."

"Please, would you come with me?" He knew they didn't understand the urgency of his request. "Right away?"

The man, who had identified himself as Burke Edwards, the owner of the ranch, answered. "It's almost dark and a storm's threatening. Better to wait for morning."

Holt shook his head. He couldn't wait. Lizzie would be worried sick. And Mr. Tate… "I must return." He reached for the door.

"Don't be foolish," Edwards said.

"I go with him, boss." Paquette shuffled toward a hallway. "You wait. I get things."

Edwards groaned. "I better go along, too, just to make sure you get there safely."

Holt shifted from one foot to the other as Paquette got ready and Edwards ducked out to saddle the horses. Finally they were mounted and on their way.

But before long he began to wonder if he should have listened to Edwards's advice. The snow started, turning the air before him into a wall of white, the road disappearing in the darkness and swirling snow.

Chapter Fourteen

Lizzie left her father's side to stare out the window.

"You think he's lost?" Emma's voice shrilled across Lizzie's nerves. She forced herself to still her worrying hands and speak calmly.

"No, dearest. I'm sure he'll be back soon."

"It's dark out."

And snow had started to fall. Or rather to blow. So strong it didn't seem to touch the ground, violently swirling in the air. *God, please keep him safe.*

She returned to Pa and resumed sponging, not knowing what else to do.

The door rattled and she jerked about. But it was only the wind. With shaking hands, she returned her attention to her task. It happened again and again, and each time she had to stop herself from bolting to the door. As the hours ticked by the room grew more and more empty.

The door rattled again. Only this time the handle also jiggled. She sprang forward, spilling water on her feet and not even caring as she threw open the door.

"Holt!" Joy she could not disguise filled her voice. "Holt, you must be freezing. Come in." She tugged at his sleeve.

"I brought help." He could barely form the words, his lips stiff with cold.

Lizzie tore her gaze from Holt's face and saw a tiny woman at his side.

"This is Paquette," he said.

"Thank God you're here! Please, come in and get warm."

"I not be cold." The woman shuffled in, shed a fur cape and went straight to Pa's side. She rubbed her hands to take the chill off of them then touched his forehead. "He be sick long time."

Even though it wasn't a question, Lizzie answered. "Yes."

"He very weak now."

Frighteningly so. Lizzie hovered at the end of Pa's bed, her stomach bouncing from pillar to post as she watched and waited. Holt shed his coat and stood at her side. She welcomed his comforting presence.

Paquette suddenly nodded. "I fix." She opened a leather pouch and pulled out an array of dried herbs. "I need hot water." Lizzie sprang forward to help.

A few minutes later Paquette had produced a noxious smelling liquid. "He drink this. All it. He start get better."

"How will he drink? He's unconscious."

Paquette touched Pa's cheeks and neck then she bent close. "Mister, open your eyes."

Lizzie gasped as Pa did so.

"You drink." Paquette lifted his head and held the cup to his lips. He swallowed three times.

"Good." She turned to Lizzie. "You see he drink all." She handed Lizzie the cup. "I be done." She sat at the table.

Emma, who had refused to go to bed until Holt returned, stared at her.

Paquette stared right back. Then she smiled. "You be nice girl."

The woman had brought something to help Pa. Holt was

safe and sound. The relief made her dizzy. Lizzie's lungs emptied so fast her legs bent. Holt caught her around the waist. She knew she should pull away. Stand on her own two feet. But she'd stood on her own for so long… She welcomed his steadying arm, but how long would he be here to offer it?

Chapter Fifteen

A wild rush of emotions drove the cold from Holt's body as he held Lizzie. Relief, concern and swirling hope all tangled with one another until he couldn't begin to say what he felt.

"Give more drink," Paquette said.

Holt steadied Lizzie, not releasing her until he was sure she wasn't going to fold like a towel dropped on the floor.

She pulled in a long breath then moved to her father's side and held the cup to his lips. He roused enough to drink some more.

The night deepened. Emma crawled into bed without being told…mostly because no one thought to tell her. Paquette wrapped her fur around herself and slept near the stove. Edwards had taken the horses to the barn and said he would wait there. Only Holt and Lizzie remained awake, giving Mr. Tate the dreadful smelling drink and watching desperately for signs that he was getting better.

He sweated profusely, which Paquette said was a good sign. Then, toward the thin dawn, he opened his eyes.

"Lizzie," he murmured. "There's a bad taste in my mouth."

She laughed and gave him water. After he drank, he closed his eyes with a contented sigh, the fever broken.

Lizzie sagged and Holt caught her. Tremors rattled her

teeth. He wrapped his arms about her and held her tight, absorbing the tremblings with his body. She clung to him, filling him with a sweet, terrifying knowledge. He loved her. When he left he would leave behind his heart.

And he would have to go. Staying would bring about nothing but his own death. Perhaps even endanger the lives of Lizzie and her family. Perhaps at some future date God would see fit to allow his name to be cleared. But until then his love was a worthless thing....

She clutched his shirt front and lifted her face to him. "I was so scared. What would we do if he...?" She swallowed back the word.

"Hush, God has answered our prayers."

The fear in her eyes shifted. Her gaze drove into his soul, searching out his hidden feelings. He tried to mask them, tried to resist the deep longing that rose within him—and failed at both. He bent his head and caught her mouth with his own. The kiss was barely a touch, but he would carry the taste of her sweet mouth beneath his for the rest of his life.

Then Paquette stirred and they sprang apart. She rolled up her fur and shuffled to Mr. Tate's side to touch his forehead and run her fingers down his neck. "He be better. Feed him plenty good food. Keep warm."

Emma scrambled down from the loft. Checked on her pa. "He's better?"

Paquette patted Emma's head. "He soon be telling you to mind manners."

They all laughed, as much from relief as amusement.

A few minutes later Edwards came in. "The snow has stopped but it's frightfully cold."

"You're welcome to stay," Lizzie said.

"Only until the sun climbs higher. No telling when it will turn worse."

Holt knew he should be making the same announcement.

Get going while it was still possible. He had fulfilled his promise to Mr. Tate, he owed them nothing.

But now something stronger than his honor held him here. An emotion so fierce it would keep him with Lizzie at least until he was sure Mr. Tate could take care of Lizzie and her sister again. Even if it meant his life.

Chapter Sixteen

Paquette and Mr. Edwards left early that morning, and as the day wore on, Pa steadily grew stronger. Lizzie's happiness knew no bounds, magnified as it was by Holt's presence.

His kiss had affected her deeply. Never had she felt this way before…full of a joy that danced across her senses.

She tried to temper it with reason. After all, he had made no promises. Over and over she caught him staring out the window with a faraway look in his eyes, and she knew he had one foot out the door and she had no claim on him.

Yet she wondered how she would manage when he left. Certainly Pa would soon be able to spend a few hours in the store. And God willing, be able in time to take over the outside chores.

But it wasn't the work that would make her miss Holt. It was the loneliness in her soul that hovered in the background. For a moment she considered suggesting she go with him when he left. Her heart leapt at the idea, but her head reminded her that her family needed her here.

Holt stepped through the door. "It's bright and sunny today. After that storm, I reckon the good weather will last a few days."

Something in his voice screeched along her nerves and

she took her time drying her hands and facing him, as if by delaying she could avoid what he had to say.

He waited until her gaze finally met his, let her see his regret as well as his resolve. "I'll be leaving in the morning."

Only by holding her breath was she able to bite back a cry. She counted to three. Then ten. Eventually she spoke, hoping her voice wouldn't reveal the depth of her pain. "You're more than welcome to stay."

He nodded. "I know. But I can't." He reached for her hands and drew her to the table, urged her to sit and pulled a chair to her side. "I am a wanted man, Lizzie."

The statement was so ridiculous that she felt a giggle tickling her throat.

"I'm accused of rustling cows and there are people who will testify that I've done it."

"How absurd. Why would they say such a thing?"

He cupped her face in his palm and gave her a look so full of tenderness her vision blurred. "Lizzie, you are sweet. How do you know I'm not guilty?"

Heat burned her cheeks and she was sure they must flash a telltale red. She'd spoken on pure instinct but she had no doubt of his innocence. "You are a God-fearing man. You would not steal. Tell me what happened?"

He trailed his fingers down her cheeks. His gaze lingered on her eyes with delightful pleasure that filled her insides with sweet music. "I rented some land and started to gather up a herd of cows. The big rancher next to my land kept reporting his cows were going missing, claimed they'd been stolen. It wasn't me, but someone framed me. Produced several witnesses who said they saw me branding a steer that belonged to my neighbor. Frontier justice would see me hanged. I decided I didn't much care for that sort of justice and headed for the Canadian border."

"But you stopped here. Why?" It put him in so much danger she dare not consider it.

"You needed help. I made a promise." He stroked her cheek. "And I don't regret it one bit." He kissed her, so full of tenderness and unspoken love that she ached clear through.

"I...I know you have to go. But...I could go with you."

His grin was crooked. "You can't leave Emma and your father. Our lives must go in different directions from here." His voice sliced through her insides, echoing her own painful conclusion.

"I don't want you to leave, but I understand you have to."

If only there were some way she could keep morning from coming.

Chapter Seventeen

Holt pushed from his sleep to the sound of a thousand stampeding animals. He shook his head. The walls of the little room in the livery barn where he slept groaned. In a flash he'd pulled on his boots and shrugged into his coat before he rushed to open the door. A blast of wet wind chilled him and he slammed the door shut. But he'd seen enough to know a snowstorm was sweeping down the street, the snow so thick he couldn't see the buildings on the other side.

"Well, I can't leave now," he muttered. He couldn't find one bit of regret at the knowledge. Another day with Lizzie. Time to build memories to last forever.

Pulling his hat down tight and securing it with his woolen scarf, he pushed into the storm. The snow swirled, making it impossible to know where he was. It stuck to his eyelashes. But he forged onward, mentally counting the steps to the store. It should be close. He squinted into the storm, caught a flicker of golden light and made his way toward it. Crashed into the door.

Lizzie threw it open and drew him inside. "I feared you would venture out and get lost."

"This is as far as I'm going until the storm lets up."

"Then I'm glad for the storm." Her words were low, meant

only for his ears. He brushed the snow from his lashes so he could look at her better. The smile in her eyes drove away the chill from the wind.

"I'm glad, too." At least the storm meant his pursuers would not be able to make progress, either. Though he still wondered why they hadn't caught up to him by now. He could only thank God for the reprieve it allowed him.

He meant to enjoy every extra moment.

"You want to play with Miss Ellen?" Emma said.

"After breakfast," Lizzie warned, her eyes revealing amusement and regret. "She'll miss you." She kept her voice soft enough that only he heard her.

Mr. Tate was up, shaking the coffeepot. Lizzie hurried to the stove to dish up porridge. Emma sat at the table, her doll beside her bowl.

Holt leaned back and watched the scene. If only he could be part of this beyond today. He shut down the longing in his heart. Circumstances had sent him on a different course.

After breakfast they played a board game, then Lizzie brought out a photograph album and introduced him to her relatives. They sat side by side, Emma on his knee, and he leaned close, breathing in the scent of Lizzie, imprinting it and the shape of her features on his mind.

And he asked God to make the storm last forever.

Chapter Eighteen

Lizzie wished the day would never end. Having Holt at her side, knowing it could not last was bittersweet.

During the night the storm ended and the next day was sunshine, bright and warm enough to make a person happy to go out to do chores. And encourage a wanted man to leave town. Holt would be on his way today. She leaned over the pile of wood to catch her breath. He'd said he would say good-bye before he left.

She made an extra large breakfast, baked biscuits and cookies for his journey.

When he came, his eyes were drawn down at the corners. Without speaking a word, she realized how much he wanted to stay. She realized he struggled with the idea and fear gripped her.

"You must leave. I couldn't bear to see you hang. Maybe someday your name will be cleared and then…"

Pa had gone to the store to fetch some raisins. Emma dug about in her belongings in the loft, leaving them virtually alone.

"When it is, I'll be back," he said. "I wish I could give you some sort of promise…but I can't. Don't wait for me, Lizzie."

She caught a cry between her teeth. She wouldn't make this any harder.

Pa came in just as Emma scampered down the ladder. They all sat around the table and Lizzie began to serve breakfast, trying to keep her hands from shaking.

After a couple of minutes, Holt put down his fork carefully. "I'll be on my way this morning," he announced to them all.

Emma's eyes widened. "You don't have to leave."

"I'm afraid I do." He faced Pa. "There are reasons." He darted a glance at Emma as if wondering how much he should say in front of her.

Pa met his eyes then nodded. "I appreciate your help. May God be with you."

Customers trailed into the store and Pa rose to tend to them.

Lizzie went to the doorway with her father to speak to him privately. "Pa, there are men after him. He's been falsely accused of rustling and will hang if he's caught."

Holt joined her. "I assure you I'm innocent."

"I never doubted otherwise." He gripped Holt's shoulder. "We will pray for God's justice."

"I wish I could believe it will prevail."

"Son, never lose faith."

From the look on Holt's face she knew he had trouble believing in justice. Even as she did. Why would God allow a good man to be falsely accused? Why would He bring such a man into her life only to tear him away?

Pa patted her shoulder. "Go say goodbye. For now. Until God answers our prayers."

"Thank you, Pa." As her father entered the store, she grabbed Holt and drew him back to the table, filling his plate with eggs and bacon, refilling his coffee cup several times. They both recognized it as her way of delaying his departure. But he seemed content to let her.

Suddenly Pa ducked into the living quarters, pulling the adjoining door closed behind him.

At the fear on his face, Lizzie let the coffeepot slam to the table.

"There are two men out front asking after you," Mr. Tate said.

Holt bolted to his feet. "They've caught up with me."

"I didn't tell them you were here. There's no one in the store who knows. So unless they start asking around at the livery barn…"

He could still get away. But he had only a few minutes at best to escape the noose.

Chapter Nineteen

There were men on the other side of the door, ready to arrest Holt and convict him of a crime he didn't commit. He knew he had to go, but somehow Holt couldn't tear himself away from Lizzie. Couldn't get enough of drinking in her features.

She spun away. "You must go now." Lizzie handed him his coat and stuck food in a bag. "Hurry."

Emma whimpered but her father pulled her to his side. "It's time, little one. Say goodbye."

The child rushed over and threw her arms about Holt. He lifted her, pressing her face to his neck. "I'm going to miss you and Miss Ellen."

He reluctantly released her to her father's arms and turned to Lizzie. Her mouth begged him to hurry and leave; her eyes begged him to stay. If only he could. But it would cost him his life, maybe even hers. The best thing he could do was ride away and leave these people safe and sound, not at the mercy of men who would accuse them of harboring a criminal.

He continued to study Lizzie. He wanted so badly to kiss her but her father watched. "Sir, do you mind?"

Mr. Tate grinned. "Go ahead."

He kissed her, acutely conscious of his audience. "I will miss you always," he murmured.

She cupped his cheek, her eyes bright. "Go. Be safe."

His horse waited at the back door. He hooked the bag of food to the saddle and swung up. His last image before he rode away was of Lizzie with her father's arm about her. Avoiding the front of the store, where he might be seen, he headed north.

The sun shone brightly. He should make good time today. In a few more days he would be safe in the Canadian Rockies, holed up someplace for the winter.

God's justice, Mr. Tate had said, as if believing in that were enough. Where was God when Holt had been falsely accused? Why hadn't He intervened?

Had Holt ever asked? Ever expected it? Given God a chance?

But if he turned around right now and rode back to face his accusers, would he end up at the wrong end of a hangman's noose?

He realized his horse had stopped walking, as if waiting for Holt to make up his mind what he wanted. Run and save his life? Go back and maybe hang? Or maybe prove his innocence and be free to tell Lizzie what was in his heart.

Was his love for her reason enough to risk dying?

He heard a sound behind him and spurred his horse into a run.

He was gone. The words wailed through Lizzie's insides. *God, keep him safe.* She pushed thoughts of Holt aside and kept herself busy at the stove. But it was impossible. Her heart called her to go after Holt.

And yet how could she? Who would look after Pa and Emma? If she left right now, could she even catch up to him?

She sighed. How foolish to even think such things. She could not abandon her family. Not even for the sake of her heart.

Pa tended to the customers in the store. It seemed unusually busy today as people stocked up before winter really set in. He came into the room. "The mail came through." He handed her several letters. She glanced at them. All from aunts and other relatives. "Go ahead and read them. Might serve to cheer you up."

"Are those men still there?"

"They are. Asking questions of everyone."

"That's good. So long as they're out there, they aren't chasing Holt."

He squeezed her shoulder. "Pray and trust God to care for him."

She nodded. He went back to the store and she opened the first letter—from her mother's sister—and read it twice. An idea formed in her head, a chance to have everything she wanted. If she was brave enough to go after it.

Chapter Twenty

"Emma, go ask Pa if he can come here." She didn't want to go into the store and see the men who were after Holt.

Emma went to the door and called Pa.

"I'll be right there," he answered.

When he came in, she handed him the letter. "Read this."

He did so, frowning. "Your aunt has suggested that she come before. I'm just not sure about it."

"Pa, don't you see? If she's here I can go find Holt."

Pa studied her a long time. "You know she's looking for marriage?"

"But it isn't a given. She can rent a room over at Miss Sachel's. She can take care of the house and Emma while you're in the store."

Pa considered her suggestion. She could see he struggled with the idea of another woman in his home. She hoped he would understand how this would free her to be with Holt.

Finally Pa nodded. "You can write her and say she's welcome."

But by the time she did all of that... She wasn't the fastest rider in the world. She'd never catch him. "Pa, can I send someone after Holt?"

"Don't think you'd have much chance of overtaking him."

"I have to try."

He reluctantly gave his agreement. She grabbed her coat and rushed toward the livery barn, praying she'd find a good horse and rider.

She stepped inside, waited for her eyes to adjust to the dim interior, located the owner in the far corner and made her request.

"If you're looking to find me, you don't need to go to all that bother."

She spun around at the sound of Holt's voice. She opened her mouth to speak but nothing came out.

He pulled her close and kissed her nose. "I decided I am not going to ride away from what we have."

"But those men…"

"Your pa said I should trust God's justice and I'm going to."

Fear clawed up her throat. Trusting God was fine when it didn't mean Holt's life. "You could hang."

"I intend to clear my name or die trying."

"It's the die trying part that worries me."

"Are they still at the store?" She told him that they were. He took her hand and led her up the street. *Oh God, help us.*

The two strangers jolted upright as Holt stepped inside.

"You're a hard man to find," the taller one said.

Holt stood so relaxed and casual she might have thought he was visiting his brother. "I'm ready to go back."

"No need. That's why we're here. The boss discovered cows were still disappearing even after you left. Turns out his own son was stealing them. You're a free man."

Holt whooped. "Justice shall prevail." He grabbed Lizzie's hand and drew her into the living quarters, sweeping her into his arms once they were alone.

"I love you, Lizzie."

She managed to say "I love you, too, Holt," before he kissed her.

"Say that you'll marry me. Promise me?"

Lizzie smiled and nodded. "I promise."

* * * * *